THE LOCKED ROOM

A JAMES LALONDE NOVELLA

A. D. HAY

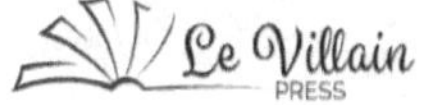

The Locked Room. A James Lalonde Novella
Copyright © A. D. Hay (2023). All rights reserved.

www.authoradhay.com

ISBN-13: 978-1-916609-02-0 (paperback)

Book cover design by Le Villain Book Covers at
levillainbookcovers.com

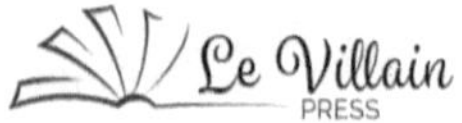

FRENCH IN THE LOCKED ROOM

Jean Dupont: *noun.* A very common French phrase used in the same way that "John Doe" or "Joe Bloggs" is used in English.

Merde: *noun.* A mild, humorous substitute for "shit."

Oh, la vache: An expression of surprise similar to "damn" or "oh my god."

ONE

SATURDAY: 11:30 A.M.

ENGLAND WAS PERFECT IN APRIL. The sun was shining, the trees were a deep green, and the sky was an exquisite shade of blue. The landscape was breathtaking and remarkably similar to France. *Don't tell the British—it won't go down too well.*

Leaning over the steering wheel of his red Peugeot, James Lalonde gawked at the gravelled driveway lined with tall, cylindrical conifer hedges sculpted to perfection, as his car idled in the middle of the open gates to Clovervale Hall. *Trimming the hedges must be a nightmare.*

The stunning scenery was the ideal distraction from that niggling feeling he got when his girlfriend, Valentine, wiggled out of the romantic work getaway. Yes, turning a work trip into a romantic getaway had been a stupid idea. But not as stupid as giving Xavier an LCD television and DVD player as a gift for the opening of his technology-free bed-and-breakfast retreat. Nevertheless, Valentine was mad that he was always working and never had time for her. In his mind, it was the perfect compromise. Wasn't that what all great relationships were built on? Unfortunately, she didn't see it that way.

So he had a romantic getaway for one, thanks to Will Thatcher's skiing accident. Somewhere in the French Alps, Will was lying in a ski resort, with a cast up to his knee.

As James made the announcement in the morning meeting a few days ago, he was shocked to discover that no one was interested in an all-expenses-paid trip to his favourite professor's new bed-and-breakfast in Oxfordshire. So, it was up to him to write a review for the *Northampton Tribune* before the weekend was up —no pressure. *Just another perk of the chief editor position.* Upon assigning himself the story, James began researching the estate and the history of the home's architectural evolution. As nerdy as it sounded, it was a rather enjoyable four hours.

The hairs on his arms stood on end as the vehicle's air-conditioning unit struggled to pump air around the tiny three-door car. He was embarrassed to admit he didn't like the heat. Anything above twenty-two degrees was insufferable. That was one of the bonuses of living in England. Summer was five days long, maybe ten at the most, in a good year. Or as he liked to describe it, a bad year. He turned the AC dial back to the first setting.

Lifting his foot off the accelerator, James inched

his car along the drive. The gravel crunched underneath the tyres as he soaked in his new surroundings. Out of nowhere, a fluffy grey English Shorthair cat sauntered across the beige stones as if it had not a care in the world.

James slammed his foot on the brake pedal as he watched the feline display a rebellious distaste for order and the rules. The cat was clearly French and out of place in a world where the queue was everything. Pausing in the middle of the driveway, the cat glanced up at him with an innocent expression in its bright yellow eyes. With his heart pounding, James shook his head. Perhaps out of curiosity, the cat ambled towards the car, jumped up on the bonnet, and strolled across. James cringed as he listened to the clicking of the cat's paws against the metal. The cat was a daredevil.

After dragging the shifter into Park, James applied the handbrake and got out of the car, leaving the driver's door open. With a sigh, he strolled around the door to the bonnet. His white sneakers scuffed against the stones, startling a bird in a nearby tree. The cat meowed then sat, claiming its newfound property. *Typical.*

He reached across the bonnet and picked up the cat, who looked up at him with a hint of defiance in its eyes. James returned to the car and climbed inside, still cradling the cat. After he closed the door, he placed the cat in the passenger seat. The feline meowed at him.

James shrugged. 'Sorry, but you can't be trusted to stay off the driveway.'

Loud honks from the car behind caused James to jump in his seat. He glanced up into the rearview mirror, and a tall man with rimless spectacles and dark-brown skin came into view. Gesturing at James with the classic one-finger salute, the man honked his horn again then pulled his smartphone out of the inside pocket of his tweed jacket—the uniform of the university professor. The man looked like he was about to blow a valve. He was going to struggle with the technology-free retreat-style bed-and-breakfast. *Does he even know?*

James took his foot off the brake and cruised along the drive. As he reached the courtyard, James gazed up at the heritage-listed manor house. Its impressive limestone walls with stone mullion windows towered over him like a fortress. Professor Xavier Watson had undersold the bed-and-breakfast. James was desperate to walk the halls of the beautiful building. Valentine was missing out. Then he realised. He had morphed into his grandfather. No wonder she hadn't wanted to come. James chuckled as he recalled his grandmother's account of wandering around the French countryside, touring four chateaux in one day. He would never forget the wild expression in her eyes as she recounted the traumatising sixteen-hour trip. James missed his grandparents—the home-cooked meals, the hugs, the intrusive questions, and the cigarettes. Smoking was a terrible habit—one that he shared—but a certain nostalgia was attached to the smell. His grandparents were far away in central western France, and he was there at the bed-and-breakfast.

Professor Xavier Watson, a tall, thin man with a bald, shiny head and a thick layer of fluffy grey hair on the sides, knocked on the passenger window. Xavier pointed at the cat and beamed. James smiled. The story was going to write itself.

TWO

———

THE SMELL of freshly cut grass mixed with a faint mossy aroma lingered in the breeze as the late-morning sun burnt the back of his neck. James had spoken too soon—it was getting hot, unusually hot for that time of year. Sweat dripped down the back of his legs. Wearing jeans had been a mistake. After inspecting his car for several minutes, the rebellious feline dashed across the stones and into the manor house. A loud *ding* echoed through the foyer of Clovervale Hall and out of the open door. Standing on the drive next to his parked car, James watched Professor Xavier Watson roll his suitcase along the gravelled driveway. There was no use arguing with Xavier. It would be fruitless and disappointing. Watching the ageing professor handle his luggage made him feel like an obnoxious jerk who clicked his fingers at waiting staff or rang bells in empty receptions while the staff struggled with the demands of other guests. He winced as a bead of sweat dripped down his back and soaked into the cotton of his light-blue polo shirt.

Another *ding* echoed through the foyer. James cringed. The tweed jacket-wearing, smartphone-wielding man's impatience was wearing thinner by the second. *What could be so urgent that the man can't wait a minute or two?*

Loud footsteps drew near.

Standing centimetres away from the doorframe and on the edge of a large, fraying, red, white, and blue Persian rug, the man cleared his throat.

'Xavier, sorry to bother you.' The man pushed his spectacles up the bridge of his nose as he leaned forwards. 'I need to get back to marking papers and preparing for lectures. You know how it is.'

Xavier's posture stiffened.

Yes, the man was the most important person there, and logic dictated that an elderly man should drop everything to serve his every whim. *Time to pull out the popcorn. This is going to be good.*

'Laurence, did you not read the email I sent you?' Xavier asked with that infamous calm tone. It was the tone reserved for students caught smoking in the halls between lectures or texting in class. The tone was very familiar to James. One day during a lecture, he was typing a text to Liam but was unaware that Xavier was standing over him, reading as he typed. As James finished texting, Xavier said his name, making him jump with fright. It was nice to see he wasn't Xavier's only victim.

Laurence sighed. 'I don't have time for this. All I need is the Wi-Fi password.'

Xavier shook his head. 'There is no Wi-Fi.'

'Don't mess with me. I'm not in the mood.'

Xavier suppressed a smile. 'Clovervale Hall Bed-and-Breakfast is a technology-free haven away from the hustle and bustle of everyday life. It's a place to unwind and escape the stresses and pressures of your world.'

'Yes, I read your marketing material.' Laurence clenched his hands into a fist then relaxed his fingers. 'There's no phone reception or even 3G. My phone says no signal.'

Xavier shook his head. 'So then, if you read the material, you should know there's no Wi-Fi.'

'What about your personal Wi-Fi?' A large vein bulged in the centre of Laurence's forehead as Xavier walked by, wheeling James's suitcase.

A rock formed in the pit of his stomach. James shuffled forwards. That argument was getting out of hand. *Why is Laurence so angry?* The atmosphere surrounding the man made James uneasy. It was as if he had rage built up within him. Perhaps something happened before Laurence drove to Clovervale Hall.

'Flora and I have no need for Wi-Fi.' Xavier lifted the small suitcase by the long handle as he stepped into the manor house.

Laurence tugged at the collar of his shirt. 'Why didn't you explicitly point that out in your email?'

'Technology-free is quite explicit. It does not promise Wi-Fi or phone reception. And it will do you a world of good to not be so permanently attached to that damn thing.' Xavier stood in the middle of the foyer with Laurence towering over him.

JAMES DASHED up the limestone stairs and into the large entrance hall. Its polished timber floors creaked underneath the Persian rug as he made a beeline to the squabbling duo. The fluffy grey feline lazily waltzed across the room's length, rubbing against the white walls under the large window that overlooked the drive and front lawn.

After grabbing Laurence by his left bicep, James dragged him to the cast-iron fireplace, nestled in the corner of the room behind two bordeaux-coloured armchairs and a round antique side table laden with magazines.

'Why are you getting physical with an elderly man?' James stared at Laurence, hoping to reason with him.

Xavier gasped as he propped against the large round table in the centre of the room. 'I'm not elderly.'

James rolled his eyes. 'You're in your seventies. You're not young anymore, and you have a heart condition. So brawls over Wi-Fi are out of the question.'

'That's ageism,' Xavier snapped.

Xavier was just as bad as his grandfather. Won't accept help of any kind, check. In denial about his age, check. Same vocabulary, check. *Do all elderly men receive a bonus handbook in the mail?*

James stared into Laurence's eyes. There was so much built-up anger behind those deep-brown irises. 'And what were you planning on doing? Knocking out a man in his seventies over Wi-Fi?'

Laurence clenched his jaw. 'Of course not. That's ridiculous.'

So Laurence knows he's being a jerk. Interesting.

The clearing of a throat in the background caused all three men to turn around. Standing in the open doorway to the library hall was Flora Watson. Her dark-brown shoulder-length hair shone under the lights. Not a single grey hair was in sight. As she smiled, deep laughter lines appeared around her sparkling blue eyes. Short, thin, and elegant, Flora was beautiful. She walked like a bird gliding over a pond. And she refused to be addressed by her formal title of professor, which was unusual in the academic world. Because of her down-to-earth approach, she'd been a popular professor at All Saints College in Oxford back in the day. Her course was so popular that there was a waiting list for her subject. To James's disappointment, he got wait-listed. Instead, he took Dr Manesh Warren's Introduction to English Language and Literature class.

'James, I must thank you for babysitting my husband and Laurence Weybourne,' Flora said with a thick southern accent. 'Apparently, you can't leave them alone for a second.' Flora raised her eyebrows at Laurence. 'Your room is ready now. Follow me.'

FIVE MINUTES LATER, a loud creak echoed through the entrance hall as Laurence Weybourne and Flora ascended the stairs in the library hall. Xavier grumbled at the sound as he trekked towards the antique desk laden with an old iMac G3, a matching transparent keyboard, and a gigantic spotted mug filled with pens. James was popping pimples when that computer first came on the market. He remembered the day his grandfather, Dr Francois Lalonde, had brought home an iMac G3 one evening after work. The inspiration for his grandfather's purchase came after retrieving a plastic, partially transparent *A* key from the stomach of a *Jean Dupont* during an autopsy. His grandmother, Dr Valerie Lalonde, had rolled her eyes at her husband's latest gadget as he pulled it out of the box and set it up. To her dismay, Francois was always an early adopter of tech. James suppressed a chuckle at the thought as Xavier punched the keyboard with his index fingers.

With a groan, Xavier glanced up over his wire-framed spectacles. 'I heard that. You know, I still have my hearing and the use of all my faculties in my grand old age.'

James sighed.

'I hope some young punk calls you old one day.' Xavier stared at the screen.

Two thick crossway beams towered above James as he wandered around the entrance hall. A dull *creak* from the oak flooring cried out as he inched towards the black cast-iron fireplace. Judging by the contents inside, the fireplace had recently been used.

He flipped through the pile of *Strong Words* magazines on the round side table. Reading about what to read was a little self-referential, but seeing the periodicals there didn't surprise him. Xavier was obsessed with books, and "obsession" was putting things mildly. In his years as a professor, Xavier had always been surrounded by books, both fiction and nonfiction. They were scattered around his office. Upon entering the manor house, James had expected to see stacks of books in every room. But Flora must have put her foot down and limited the books to the library. James sauntered past the large round table in the centre of the expansive foyer, which bore a large vase swelling with ivory English roses, giving the room its fragrance, which included a mixture of cedar and orange blossom.

'Here it is.' Xavier peered up from behind the iMac, leaned down, opened the drawer to his right, and pulled out a key. 'I found your room. It's room three. Unfortunately, you don't have your own bathroom. But the room is large and overlooks the front lawn. It has a pleasant view.' Xavier stood and ambled around the desk and across the foyer. 'There are lots of bathrooms. Unfortunately, due to the heritage grade of the house, we couldn't change things, like giving each room a bathroom and stuff like that.' Xavier leaned in conspiratorially. 'The heritage people are a nightmare to work with.'

Far off in the background, a car door slammed and echoed through the entrance. Xavier scurried across the room and glanced out the large window. A woman with long red hair and oversized Chanel sunglasses strutted across the gravel, dragging a small suitcase behind her.

Xavier glanced at the ceiling. 'Oh, Flora,' he mumbled.

James tapped him on the shoulder. 'I can find my way to my room. They're numbered, right?'

Xavier grimaced and tossed his head from side to side. 'Okay, you're in room three.'

With a sigh, Xavier surrendered the key as a worried expression swept across his face. The old man focused his gaze out the window and muttered to himself as the grey cat jumped onto the windowsill and stared out.

Holding the giant antique key with an ornate decorative tassel attached, James strolled across the foyer to the open door and into the library hall as he searched for his room. Then he paused. Xavier had his suitcase.

THREE

AFTER AN EMBARRASSING FIVE minutes of arguing with Xavier in front of the mysterious redhead, James commandeered his suitcase and strolled through the foyer and into the library hall. It sported a high ceiling and off-white walls with intricate carvings. This section of the house felt like it was made in a completely different era than the entrance, which seemed more straightforward in its design. *Perhaps the family that built the property expanded it after coming into a fortune.*

He strolled across a second Persian rug. In its centre was another large round table, that one lined with hardback picture books featuring the English countryside and castles. He climbed the beautiful antique brown grand staircase while admiring the Tudor-inspired tapestry that hung on the wall above the off-white marble fireplace. The stairs turned a sharp corner and grew steeper. He was out of breath. *How embarrassing. Xavier was fitter than he appeared. Is it time for a gym membership? Not today.*

The stairs creaked in protest as he continued to climb. He wheezed as he reached the top. To his dismay, the first room at the top of the stairs was room two, and to the right and down the hall was the master bedroom. A little farther down the hall, he passed a dressing room turned cleaner's closet and a bathroom, then he found bedroom three. Nestled in the corner of the windowsill opposite his room was a pile of paperback novels. *Perhaps Xavier won that fight after all.*

After slipping the antique key into the lock, James rotated the key and listened to the loud click, then he turned the knob and pushed the door open. In the centre of the room was a large window dressed with a pair of thick, heavy red drapes that reminded him of the Persian rugs from downstairs. Between the curtains was a box seat covered in the same fabric. Opposite that was an Elizabethan four-poster bed. Xavier wasn't kidding when he'd said his son-in-law and daughter spent years renovating the manor house with a team of experts.

James strolled past the open antique writing bureau, glanced in the large wooden mirror at the bags under his eyes, then continued to the large window and looked out at the front lawn. His room resembled a reconstructed Elizabethan-age bedroom in a museum. At any moment, a security guard would appear out of nowhere and scold him for jumping the sectioned-off rope.

His story would be easy to write. The house and grounds were spectacular, and the bed-and-breakfast was too cheap. He had to mention the room prices to Xavier. James lifted his small wheeled suitcase onto the box seat and admired the gardens. He pulled out his smartphone and made a few notes on an app. As he typed, the words "no signal" glared up at him from the top right-hand corner of the screen.

————

ONE HOUR LATER, James stalked the narrow hallways of the first floor of Clovervale Hall, pausing every few moments to photograph the interior architecture. He cringed as a *ding* echoed through the house. Two muffled voices whispered from within the foyer.

After checking the photos on his smartphone, James walked up the hall. As he reached the huge fourth window, James leaned on the oak panelling and gazed at the topiaries. Far off in the centre of the dark-green hedge maze stood a familiar tweed jacket-wearing man and a woman with long red hair and oversized dark sunglasses in an animated discussion. Arms flailed, fingers pointed, then Laurence strutted around as if deep in thought. The mysterious redhead stood her ground.

With his smartphone in hand, James tapped the home button and opened the camera app. Next, he tapped the video option and pressed the large red button as he watched the drama unfold.

Laurence strutted to the woman with the oversized dark sunglasses and pointed at her. By then, that vein must have been bulging at the centre of his forehead. Laurence leaned over and poked her shoulder, shaking her. He'd just struck a woman. The redhead jolted back. They froze. Out of nowhere, she slapped Laurence across the face, turned around, and stormed off through the maze and towards the manor house.

As she exited the maze in a rage, she flounced across the patio between the two wings of Clovervale Hall and disappeared.

Laurence stood still in the centre of the maze, almost as if frozen in time. It seemed as though Laurence had never experienced someone standing up to him in that way before. After all, he was the one who'd got physical first. James glanced down at the screen, struck the button to end the recording, slipped his smartphone into his back pocket, and strolled up the hall.

Through the wall separating the two sections of the house, James heard the word "idiot" muttered by a female voice, followed by a series of dull thuds. *Did she just throw something?* A loud *thump* boomed through the upper level—she was throwing something heavier and more violently than before.

From the foyer, three *dings* in quick succession

echoed through Clovervale Hall. James listened as a voice sighed. Not a single movement was heard. *Is no one coming to serve the guest?* It wasn't like Xavier to be scared of angry or antagonistic people.

FOUR

———

SATURDAY: 12:42 P.M.

CURIOUS ABOUT THE source of the aggressive bell ringing, James headed down the library hall staircase. The floorboards creaked as the library door opened then closed. *Is someone hiding in the library? Interesting.*

Another *ding* cried out from the entrance hall. James rolled his eyes as he sauntered down the stairs, across the library hall, and into the foyer.

A middle-aged woman with a snow-white pixie cut stood in the centre of the room, her oversized designer tote flung open on the antique table next to the prehistoric G3. She rubbed her reddened shoulders. The colour was no doubt the result of not wearing sunscreen in the recent hot weather. It was a sight that was all too familiar to James, as he lunched outside during the week near the *Northampton Tribune* office. *Why don't the Brits wear sunscreen?*

She cleared her throat. 'You certainly took your time.'

Perched in her shadow was a voluptuous woman in her early twenties with large, deep-brown eyes and ruler-straight long black hair that touched the waistband of her oversized floral-print shirtdress. The young woman stared at the floor. It was as if she hoped to go unnoticed and thus be uninvolved in the middle-aged woman's shenanigans.

'You do realise that I am a popular food critic, and I don't like to be kept waiting like this, especially if you want a decent review that will attract'—she glanced over her designer spectacles—'paying clients?'

James paused and smirked as he reached the two-drawer antique desk. 'If that's the case, then you would've noticed that I'm not Professor Xavier Watson but another guest.'

She groaned. 'Sybil Curry,' she barked with a thick American accent.

James shrugged.

'You can check me in.' Sybil pointed at the iMac G3. 'It shouldn't be too hard. That thing is over the hill.'

Against his better judgement and to double-check that she was nowhere near his room, James clicked the round mouse. The password screen lit up. Out of habit, James lifted the keyboard. Underneath was a password written in handwriting messier than that in his grandfather's pathology reports back in the early nineties when he took work home.

He typed in the password, pressed Enter, and waited as the screen slowly unveiled. In the search bar of the Clovervale Hall MS-DOS-inspired database, he entered the woman's name.

'Well?' she scoffed.

James bit his lip to stifle a laugh at Xavier's password for the computer— "battle-axe."

Sybil cleared her throat and brushed her hand along her pale-pink sleeveless blouse. 'Have you found my room yet?'

The page slowly loaded to reveal Sybil's details and her room allocation. *Merde—it is not good news.*

James tore his eyes away from the horror unfolding on the screen and stared at Sybil. 'You're in room four.'

He tugged on the black cast-iron handle of the drawer then pulled out the antique key for room four. As James handed over the key, lying in her designer tote on top of a pile of purses—and other accessories that he didn't recognise—was a small silver revolver with an ornate white handle and a small speed loader with six rounds. The angry food critic had a gun and a short fuse. On top of that, she was right next door to him, only a thin wall away.

'And you, ma'am.' James peered over Sybil's shoulder.

The young woman murmured something inaudible.

'She's shy,' Sybil announced. 'Her name is Honey Knowles. She's my assistant and should have her own room next door to mine.'

James entered the name into the search bar and brought up Honey's details. Inwardly, he groaned at the results. His least favourite food critic, whom he had never heard of until then, wasn't going to like them.

'Ah, you're in room seven.' James reached into the open drawer, pulled out the key, and handed it over. Honey stared at the floor as Sybil snatched the key out of his hand.

'That's not acceptable,' Sybil snapped. 'I asked for side-by-side rooms.'

As Sybil protested, James searched the desk for a map, and Flora waltzed into the entrance hall.

'Sybil.' Flora smiled as she embraced the unruly guest. 'Honey is in room seven, which is just around the corner. Rooms five and six are in a different section of the house, which is not accessible from room four. I thought that wouldn't be appropriate for your situation. And you have your own bathroom. Not all guests have that luxury.'

Seizing the opportunity, James slipped out from behind the desk, dashed across the entrance hall, and disappeared out of sight.

A lone thought swirled in his mind as he returned to his room. So, he was staying next to a mad woman with a gun. And how did Sybil come to have an expensive-looking Smith & Wesson? The United Kingdom had strict firearm laws. That meant that either she'd jumped through the necessary hoops, or it was an illegal weapon.

FIVE

———

SATURDAY: 2:07 P.M.

AFTER LISTENING through the thin walls as Sybil muttered to herself about the so-called problems with her accommodation for just under an hour, James decided to tour the grounds and take more photos. Fifteen minutes later, he trekked through the maze. Far off in the distance, a dark-grey cloud loomed, threatening to spoil the day. The aromatic hedges of the maze cast James's mind back to his childhood, when his grandfather took him on his first visit to Chateau de Villandry in central France. While the gardens of Clovervale Hall were nothing compared to the intricate hedging of Villandry, it was remarkable nonetheless. *If it rains, then perhaps it'll bring the temperature down a few degrees.*

As he reached the edge of the maze, off to the right was a path leading to the greenhouse, summerhouse, and the pool-and-spa pavilion. It was far off on the other side of the property, but according to the website that Xavier's son-in-law had built, it boasted a full-length swimming pool, sauna, and spa treatment facilities. James could do with a massage and a trip to the sauna. The current temperature caused him to sweat through his light-blue polo, creating wet armpit patches. Thankfully, Valentine wasn't around to witness it.

———

SEVEN MINUTES LATER, he opened the pool house door and strolled across the beige tiles. He paused. Swimming laps in the full-length pool, alternating between freestyle and backstroke, was a tanned man with a Photoshop-perfect body that bore a plethora of mismatched tattoos exclusively contained to his torso. If he wore a shirt, the artwork would all be concealed from view. *Are tattoos placed together supposed to follow a theme? Or is it a case of getting one whenever inspiration strikes? Great, I'm staring—merde.*

The tall, muscular man stopped and folded his arms along the pool's edge. 'If you could refrain from taking photos, I'd appreciate it.'

James closed his eyes and sighed—he had forgotten to pull out his smartphone and take photos of the grounds. *I'm an idiot.*

'Look, I'm happy to take a selfie with you. But just not now.' The man groaned.

Who does this guy think he is? A famous movie

star? Everyone in the place was crazy, angry, or delusional. *What does this say about me? Do I fit right In?*

He nodded as he sauntered around the pool towards the sauna, treatment rooms, and changing area.

'I just want a bit of privacy, that's all,' the man said as James wandered off.

James glanced over his shoulder. 'I wasn't taking a photo of you. And second, to me, you're just a random guy in a pool, someone who spent too long in the gym.'

'Well, that's rude.' The man overemphasised his posh British accent as he turned and stalked through the water towards the other side of the pool, where James was standing. Mister "Don't Look at Me" was, at the most, eight percent body fat and over six feet tall. And annoying. Thank God Valentine hadn't come with him. The last thing he needed was to compete for her attention with that vain cretin.

James shook his head. 'Obviously, I don't have a camera out. And I don't know who you are. This is a public place. I'm free to explore the grounds as I please.'

The man nodded then combed his wet hair back. 'So, you don't recognise me, then?'

Build a bridge, buddy.

'I'm Christopher Page.' Christopher paused as if waiting for something. 'I play the archaeologist in the Nic Vane movies.'

James shrugged. 'Sorry, I haven't seen those films,' he lied.

James slipped his hands into his pockets and trekked towards the treatment rooms, leaving the diva standing in the middle of the pool, speechless. He dared not look back. The actor James had watched in the Nic Vane films seemed younger, and there was something very different about his face. Maybe he'd had some plastic surgery. Christopher was almost unrecognisable.

Once James approached the closed door, he turned the handle—locked. So much for starting the afternoon off with a massage.

'She's off sick,' Christopher said as he passed by, rubbing his wet face into a fluffy white towel as he made his way towards the changing rooms.

Then James realised he was trapped in a technology-free bed-and-breakfast, so work wasn't an option. For the first time in months, he had the afternoon to himself. And he was paralysed with indecision.

SIX

———

AFTER A SWIM, a session in the sauna, and a relaxing few minutes in the hot tub, James trekked through the pool and spa pavilion as he wore a white polo shirt, navy chinos, and white canvas sneakers. He couldn't believe it. For the first time in ages, he had spent more than two hours relaxing, not editing copy or managing household tasks but enjoying his free time. With a smile, he reached the front door of the pavilion with a small carryall. After throwing his wet white towel into the hamper, he opened the door and stepped out into the warm late-afternoon sun.

Across the lawn, Flora and Xavier exited the greenhouse with smears of dirt on their clothes. James waved as he sauntered towards the greenhouse. Standing in the middle of the backfield of the Clovervale Hall property, James waited for Xavier and Flora to catch up with him.

'What are you growing in there?' James called out as Xavier and Flora drew nearer.

Flora adjusted the brim of her straw hat. It was one of those hats worn by women with expensive bathing suits who never seemed to take a dip in the ocean. 'Oh, Clovervale Hall has its own vegetable patch.'

'I didn't realise that you could grow vegetables in a greenhouse. I always thought it was for tropical plants that needed heat,' James said as the three of them walked in the direction of the manor house.

Flora chuckled. 'Tell me you're an urbanite without telling me you're an urbanite.'

Xavier laughed. 'James grew up in a university city in France quite similar to Oxford, just smaller and minus the prestige.'

'Wow, thanks for the shade.' James shook his head.

'Sorry.' Flora blushed. 'It's better to grow vegetables in a greenhouse. The environment is ideal, and it keeps hungry little critters away.'

James sighed. 'I meant Xavier.'

Flora chuckled. 'Yes, my Xavier can be quite the stirrer. It's why I married him, actually.' Flora nudged Xavier. 'There's never a dull moment.'

'The University of Poitiers isn't that bad. It was founded in 1431.'

'It's no Oxford,' Xavier said with a wink.

'Xavier, stop it. Don't you remember what happened the last time the English and the French squabbled over Poitiers?' Flora bit her lip as if stifling a laugh.

James chuckled. 'I get it. You don't want a bloodbath on your back lawn or over the hedge maze.'

'Technically, Edward, the black prince, had an Anglo-Gascon force, who were French who preferred the English king over the French king, as they saw themselves as independent from France,' Xavier grumbled.

Flora shook her head. 'It was a joke, Xavier.'

Deciding to drop the debate after sensing an inevitable loss, James ambled across the lush green grass, listening to it crinkle underfoot. As they drew nearer to the hedge maze, off to the left side of the house, he spotted a plastic playhouse, bright-blue clamshell sandpit, and a child's bicycle with training wheels, all left out in the open and waiting to be played with.

James nudged Flora. 'How old is Rosaline's son now?'

'Theo is seven.' Flora sighed. 'He's big, very serious, and loves playing outside.'

Xavier walked over to the bicycle and steered it to the maze. 'Rosaline and her husband, Rupert, live off-site in Clovervale village. They're currently quarantining because little Theo has the chicken pox.'

'Not just Theo,' Flora added.

'Oh, that's right. Rosaline has it too,' Xavier mumbled as he steered the bicycle around the maze.

'Do you tend to the garden every day?'

'Yes, and sometimes, we lose track of time and end up spending two hours in the greenhouse, like we did today.' Flora shrugged. 'I like to check the vegetables every day.'

'Really?' James gestured towards the entrance to the maze and waited for Flora to enter first.

'Mostly, I'm just off with the fairies.' Flora waved her hand in the air. 'You know, daydreaming and admiring the view.'

Together, they walked through the maze, discussing all the ins and outs of owning a vegetable patch. As James drew closer to Clovervale Hall, he glanced up and spotted the grey cat perched in the window outside his room on the upper level.

Flora giggled. 'Our resident grump, Michelangelo, has taken a shine to you.'

'Like the Renaissance artist?'

'No, after the Ninja Turtle, I'm afraid.' Flora stifled a laugh. 'He came with the house. He's a stray. Xavier let Theo name him.'

'And Michelangelo likes being indoors?'

'Seems he's grown quite accustomed to the luxury of Clovervale Hall. It's his house, you see. Xavier and I are just caretakers.' Flora grinned.

James cringed at the squeak of the training wheels as Xavier steered the small bike to the corner of the terrace area between the two side wings of the manor house.

Remembering Xavier's distaste for gossip and concerned that he might overhear and scold him, James leaned in towards Flora and whispered, 'What's the deal between Xavier and Laurence? That argument this afternoon was wild, not to mention trivial.'

'That man is more wound up than an antique clock. He specialises in Mediaeval Eurasian History, which isn't a particularly taxing subject. When I first met him, I thought he was an investment banker or something similar. Xavier invited him because he thinks Laurence needs to unwind.' Flora shook her head. 'Honestly, he could do with a Prozac prescription. Or if I'd known that things were going to be like this, I would have grown a special vegetable section just for Laurence.' Flora winked.

James nodded as he bit the inside of his lip.

'You saw the fight in the maze earlier?' Flora raised her eyebrows.

'So, who is the woman?'

'Her name is Stella Truman.' Flora leaned in conspiratorially. 'If you ask me, that argument felt like a lover's quarrel. But then again, what do I know? Stella is my cousin's daughter and has just arrived in the country. So how could she possibly know Laurence? Strange, isn't it?'

'Yes.'

Xavier chuckled in the background. James glanced over at Xavier, who was pointing at the window. Michelangelo appeared to be tapping on the glass with his paw. *What is that feline up to? And do Stella and Laurence know each other? If so, how did they meet?*

James sighed. It was embarrassing to admit, but he

was becoming more interested in the melodrama than in writing a story for the *Northampton Tribune*.

SEVEN

SATURDAY: 6:44 P.M.

TWO HOURS LATER, after smelling the aroma of meat and herbs wafting through the manor house, James wandered out of his room and down the library hall staircase, his hand gliding along the smooth, polished, antique-brown oak handrail. He ambled through the halls of the manor house then into the dining room. To his surprise, he wasn't the first to arrive in the exquisite Tudor-style room. Dark wooden panelling with cross beams stretched across all four walls. A large four-part casement window spanned the far wall. The thick curtains were drawn, allowing the light of the setting sun to dart across the already laid table, brightening the room. A black cast-iron chandelier, converted to electricity towards the end of the nineteenth century, hung from the ceiling. James sauntered over to the table and pulled out the nearest chair. It was heavy. He couldn't believe he was allowed to eat at that table. It was as if he had time travelled to a bygone era.

Sybil cleared her throat and ruined his mental trip to Tudor England. Ignoring her, he gazed at the dark-stained fireplace. The intricate carvings must have taken years to create. Above the fireplace, etched into the wall was a Tudor-style painting of a woman whose image had been captured there for as long as the fireplace had existed. Sybil cleared her throat a second time. *Seriously, take a hint.*

James glanced across the table.

'The seats are assigned,' she scoffed.

James surveyed the table. Not a single place card was in sight. 'By whom? You?'

Sybil groaned. 'Just sit next to Honey. A little order never hurt anyone.'

With a sigh, James strolled around the table after realising that it was a better seat than the one he had chosen. As a bonus, the spot at the table was not opposite Sybil, and she was out of his line of sight. As he sat, Sybil jumped up from her seat, waltzed to the open door, leaned out, and glanced down the hall. Even his grandmother, who loved to host dinner parties and plan every second of the evening, didn't assign seats at a dinner table.

James smiled politely at Honey. 'So, is she always a...?' James paused as he struggled to find the right words, hoping not to come across as insensitive.

Honey blushed as she rearranged her fork and

knife on the table in front of her. 'A dictator,' she added, her soft accent overemphasising the *R*.

James chuckled. 'Do people say that about Sybil in front of you?'

'People usually say a lot worse. She can be a hard pill to swallow sometimes. But she has good intentions.' Honey shrugged, grabbed the glass with her left hand, and took a sip.

'I ran into Christopher Page in the pool.' James nodded. 'It was quite the experience. Let's just say he has an extremely healthy sense of self.'

Honey blushed again. 'OMG, I saw him walking around the upper level in just a towel. He's divine.'

James rolled his eyes. 'I'm glad my girlfriend didn't come with me.'

'You're not completely hideous.' Honey chuckled as she wrinkled her fleshy turned-up nose, which reminded him of an excellent ski slope. 'Don't be so hard on yourself.'

James shook his head. 'Is Sybil looking for someone?'

'It's just the seating thing. Sybil wants to make sure everyone sits where she wants.' Honey lifted a shoulder. 'I think she's socially anxious, and this is how she copes.'

James leaned back in his chair and glanced at the portrait above the fireplace. From that angle, he was certain it was a part of the fireplace, not just cleverly placed. The woman in the painting reminded him of images he'd seen of Anne Boleyn or Lady Jane Grey.

'What?' a high-pitched voice cried out.

Stella stood in the doorway with her hands on her hips. She seemed furious.

'Well, I thought you would be more appreciative of the seating arrangements and wanted to sit next to Laurence,' Sybil said calmly. 'You seemed quite close. That's all.'

Stella stormed across the room, yanked out the Tudor-style chair, and sat, leaving an empty seat between her and Sybil.

That went well.

Honey tapped James's forearm. 'Have you met Laurence yet?'

'Oh yes,' James whispered. 'I had to break up a fight between him and Xavier when I arrived. It was over Wi-Fi. He was steamed over something so trivial.'

'I saw him leaving the cleaner's closet, looking a little dishevelled,' Honey said in a hushed tone. 'Two hours ago. And he has a ring on a certain finger.'

'He's married?'

'According to the jewellery.'

James grimaced. 'If he's going at it with someone in the cleaner's closet, why is he so wound up? Sex gives you a rush of endorphins. And that should make him very happy.'

'Maybe it was bad.'

Contemplating the newfound information, James pondered the possibilities and focused on not asking the most obvious question. The last thing he needed was to insert himself into some drama. But if Laurence was married, why did he come alone? Then James realised that maybe he'd agreed to attend because he was meeting a lover. It made sense. Why else would a man who couldn't seem to live without Wi-Fi show up to a technology-free retreat-style bed-and-breakfast in the outskirts of Oxfordshire? Yes, it made perfect sense.

The double-action swinging door that perfectly blended in with the wall swung open as a short, stocky man with black-and-white checked trousers, a white chef's overcoat, and a thick head of salt-and-pepper hair sauntered backwards while carrying the roast beef.

Sybil gasped. 'I hope you wore a hairnet as you cooked that roast,' she said in a commanding tone.

The woman had officially missed her calling. She should've been a primary school teacher.

After turning around, the man walked to the table, placed the roast down, then pulled out a set of carving knives and sliced into the meat. The chef paused and rubbed the tip of his fleshy turned-up nose with his forearm as he stifled a groan. He rubbed his nose for a second time then returned to the carving. The man clearly needed to have a good scratch but wasn't going to get the relief he craved while in the presence of Sybil. Poor guy was in hell. And he was coping remarkably well, considering the circumstances.

'Shouldn't you do that in the kitchen?' Sybil pushed out her chin as she watched the man go about his work.

The man grumbled. 'Yes, as the head chef with over thirty years of experience, I take advice from a food blogger with an overinflated sense of self-importance,' he said as he carved the roast without looking up.

Flora scurried into the room, her arms laden with white fine bone china plates. 'Everyone, this is Gordon Norrison, our head chef. Tonight, we thought it would be nice to give you a home-cooked meal experience.' Flora walked over to Gordon and placed the plates to his right. 'So, carving the roast at the table makes sense, just like you would at home.'

As Sybil opened her mouth, Honey squeezed Sybil's hand and smiled sympathetically.

With a groan, Christopher Page strolled into the dining room, tucking his white shirt into his black trousers as he made his way to the spare seat between Sybil and Stella. He pulled out the chair and sat.

'That seat isn't for you,' Sybil said.

'I'll sit where I like,' Christopher mumbled.

Sybil leaned back in her chair. 'But that seat is for Laurence.'

'Look around.' Christopher waved his hand around the room. 'He's not even here. And who saves seats? We're not in high school.'

Flora sighed. 'Has anyone seen Laurence?'

'I'll go get him.' James jumped up and sauntered around the table and towards the door.

———

TEN MINUTES LATER, after spending five minutes knocking on Laurence's door, James searched the rest of the house to no avail. Not because he wanted to find Laurence but to get away from the faint foul stench that seemed to permeate the air from underneath the bathroom door between the cleaner's closet and his room. So far, the three bathrooms on the upper level were empty. James stood outside the water closet opposite the third bathroom on the upper level. A light shone underneath the door, but no sound came from within the room. He felt like a creep for listening to a man's private moments. But he had to get over it. Laurence was missing out on the roast beef. It looked great, and it would be a crime to miss such a meal.

James knocked on the door. 'Laurence, dinner is ready,' he announced for the fifth time in ten minutes.

But no answer came. The entire upper level felt deserted. Perhaps Laurence was ignoring him.

He repeated the knocking ritual but got no reply. Scared of what he might find, James turned the handle and pushed open the door. To his relief, the toilet was empty. Some cretin had left the light on. After turning off the light, James trekked down the stairs and checked the library, which was also empty. Admitting defeat, James returned to the dining room without Laurence.

———

AFTER JAMES ANNOUNCED that he couldn't find Laurence, Xavier dismissed his concerns and started the meal without the missing guest. No wonder Laurence was in a foul mood all the time. He was skipping meals.

The two-course dinner went by without a hitch, and not a single ounce of drama unfolded. And for the first time since James had met her, Sybil seemed happy. For dessert, Gordon served a mouthwatering *crème brûlée*. It was magnificent. The tiny dessert was flavourful but not overpowering, and the layer of hardened caramelised sugar was torched to perfection. Gordon had redeemed himself, according to Sybil. She actually said that out loud.

Once dessert was finished and the table cleared, they sat around the Tudor table and played the winter edition of Carcassonne. Because James won the first round, Christopher insisted on playing a second time. It was obvious that the man didn't like to lose. So they all retired to their rooms once the second game came to its natural end and the scores were calculated.

James had won, and Christopher fumed. To James's delight, the film star came in last, even though he'd cheated numerous times. On several occasions, James caught Christopher peeking at the facedown tiles in the pile. It was nice to see Christopher get his comeuppance. But what did that say about James? He was revelling in another man's demise—over a board game. *Could I be any more of a nerd?*

THIRTY MINUTES LATER, at six to eleven in the evening, James lay in bed, staring at the canopy, listening to Sybil complain about the smell and a feline meowing at his door. The scent could barely be detectable from her doorway, but it was putrid in his room, as if it was coming through the walls. James was surprised that Laurence wasn't complaining as well. Or maybe the cleaner's closet and its array of chemicals provided a much-needed buffer from the smell.

Outside, the rain pelted down, and the winds howled. The ceiling creaked in protest of the raging storm. The rain hadn't let up since nine o'clock, which was unusual. It felt tropical and out of place in that part of the world. But however crazy, the storm was nothing compared to the cyclone brewing a few centimetres outside James's door. At least the storm would help him drift off to sleep. But that wouldn't happen unless he did something about cyclone Sybil.

Tired of listening to the melodrama, James dragged his weary body off the bed, opened the wardrobe, pulled out the robe, and put it on as he walked to the door. James stepped past the bedside table, grabbed his smartphone, and slipped it into the large pocket in his robe.

As James sauntered out of his room, Michelangelo dashed down the hall. He sat at the top of the grand library staircase and turned his head as he continued to meow.

With his back to Sybil's verbal smackdown with Xavier, James strolled to the bathroom between the cleaner's closet and his room—the place he believed to be the source of the stench. He opened the door, stepped inside the bathroom, and sniffed. *Interesting.*

The stench didn't seem to come from the usual places. Instead, it smelt like a koala's paradise—pine and eucalyptus.

James walked out of the bathroom and toggled the handle of the cleaner's closet. It was locked.

'James.' A familiar voice called out from behind him.

He didn't need to turn. James knew exactly who it was. With a sigh, he hung his head. Then out of the corner of his eye, James spotted a pool of crimson liquid oozing out from under the door to room two—Laurence's room. *Merde.*

EIGHT

———

SATURDAY: 11:00 P.M.

NOT AGAIN. *Why do I always have to be the one to make these discoveries?* James knew exactly what he was about to find. There was no need to turn the handle. But he had to—leaving Xavier to uncover this would be despicable.

'James,' a shrill voice repeated.

'Not now!' James snapped as he sniffed the foul odour.

It was the smell of decomposition. James had smelt it once before and would never forget it.

'There's no need to be rude,' Sybil said.

James whirled around. 'So, it's okay for you to order people about and yell at the elderly, but when I do it, it's not okay.'

Sybil stepped back.

James twisted the doorknob, but it wouldn't budge—it was locked. He paused and tried to recall the last time he saw Laurence, but nothing came to mind other than the fight he'd watched from the window. *When was that?*

He reached into the pocket of the white robe he had thrown over his green-and-blue-checked pyjama trousers. James pulled out his smartphone, tapped the screen, and opened the photo app. A few clicks later, he stared at the video's metadata. The filming had ended at 12:38 p.m.

As James thought back, he failed to recall what Laurence did after the fight because he had been too busy listening to Stella's angry outburst. And to the best of his knowledge, James didn't see Laurence on any of his four trips between the pool house and Clovervale Hall.

James turned to Sybil. 'When did you last see Laurence?'

'Ah…' Sybil took another step back. 'I don't know,' she stammered.

James raised his eyebrows. 'Before dinner, you told Stella that you thought she and Laurence were close. To know that, you must have seen him.'

'That was just idle gossip.' Sybil stormed off in a huff.

'Oh dear,' Xavier said from over James's shoulder. Standing to his right, the old man went white as he gazed at the floor.

'Do you remember when you last saw Laurence?' James asked.

Xavier nodded. 'I see why you're asking. The stench is quite strong.'

'And the room is locked.'

Xavier continued to stare at the crimson pool on the carpet. 'Just after midday, he left the house, and I saw him leave the library around three. But I saw him only briefly.' Xavier shrugged. 'I'll go get the master key. Maybe I'll stop by and ask Gordon if Laurence ordered a snack via room service. Gordon had to stay in a room because the road was flooded.'

James turned the handle once more. He threw his weight into the door, but it wouldn't budge. A sharp pain shot through his shoulder. As he stepped back and winced, Honey gasped from the end of the hallway. Glancing up the corridor, he forced a polite smile at her as she stood with her hand over her mouth, wearing nothing but an oversized Mariners T-shirt.

'You should stay in your room,' James said as he trekked to his own.

He opened the door and sprinted across the room to the large window. Kneeling on the box seat next to a pile of pillows, he separated the heavy red drapes and opened the window. The rain beat against the glass panels and drenched him as he leaned out and gazed down the side of the house. The two windows to his right appeared to be closed. So, if no one could enter via the door because it was locked, and the window was closed, it couldn't be murder. James gazed at the narrow ledge that skirted the length of the building. It was only a few centimetres wide. There was no way someone could enter the room via the outside of the building, even in perfect weather.

Was Laurence depressed enough to end his life? The man didn't seem depressed. Angry, yes, but not suicidal. But then again, it was hard to know what was going on inside someone's mind unless they shared it.

Loud knocks interrupted James's train of thought. He leaned inside the room, closed the window, drew the curtains, then got up from the box seat. Sybil stood in the open doorframe. As he strolled towards the door, her ghost-like appearance came into view.

'It's gone,' she gasped.

'What?'

'Don't play dumb with me. I know you saw it in my bag when you checked me in.'

NINE

———

JAMES GLANCED at the wall to his left as he contemplated Sybil's revelation. *So, she brought a gun, and it's now missing. And Laurence is dead.* Actually, he didn't know that for sure, but a pool of blood was seeping out from under the door to room two.

He raised his eyebrows. 'Please tell me you kept it in the safe along with the small speed loader.'

Sybil stammered.

'Are you trying to tell me you didn't leave it in the safe?'

'N-No,' Sybil stuttered. 'I brought it for protection. What use is it if it's in a safe?'

James sighed. 'So, when did you last see the gun?'

'Her name is Annie.'

'You named your gun?' James rolled his eyes.

'That's not relevant. There are more pressing matters.' Sybil cocked her head. 'It was definitely in my bag while I was on the plane.'

James bit his lip. 'You boarded a flight with the gun in your bag?'

'I don't fly commercial, dear,' Sybil scoffed. 'And there are procedures to be followed. I got it back after the flight and placed it in my handbag.'

James grimaced. 'I checked you in around twelve forty-five p.m. So that's the last time you saw... er, Annie?'

'Yes, that's correct.'

James shook his head.

'Obviously, the man offed himself with my gun.' Sybil stormed down the hall, leaving James standing in his room in shock.

Could that woman be any more insensitive?

———

FIVE MINUTES LATER, James strolled down the corridor and knocked on the door of room two. He called out Laurence's name then leaned in, careful not to disturb the blood. He pressed his ear against the door and listened. All he could hear was the gentle, rhythmic ticking of a clock from far off in the distance and meowing from the windowsill to his far left.

A familiar voice let out an exasperated sigh. James glanced at the grand staircase and watched Xavier lean against the bannister, clutching the keys.

'Gordon is counting sheep,' Xavier said breathlessly. 'I tried rousing him, but he's not waking up.'

Xavier ambled the short distance from the top of the stairs to the door to room two. He held out a finger then strolled to the cleaner's closet and unlocked it with a key. A few seconds later, he rummaged through the closet and reemerged with a box of gloves.

'Just in case.' He held them out to James. 'Hopefully, he's just injured and his wounds aren't fatal.'

After putting on the gloves, James grabbed the master key and unlocked the door. As he pushed the door open, he was met with resistance. James fumbled around and flicked on the light. Popping his head through the sixteen-centimetre gap between the frame and door, James spotted Laurence lying faceup with a bullet wound in his forehead. James surveyed the room. The layout of Laurence's room was similar to his. But no gun was in sight. A pile of papers was scattered across the room. As James followed the trail, he noticed the documents originated from the small stack on the box seat under the large window. He pulled his smartphone out of the pocket of his robe and took a few photos of the scene.

James leaned out of the room as he slipped the phone back into his pocket. 'He's behind the door.'

'There's no way I can get in through that gap.' Xavier shook his head. 'I'm too old to be shimmying through gaps.'

Now, he's too old. So I guess age has its advantages.

James sighed and squeezed through the ajar door, careful not to push it and move Laurence's body.

James held his breath. His days of vomiting at crime scenes were over, but he still felt queasy. He froze as he stared at Laurence's dull skin—its former dark-brown colour had a greyish hue.

As he regained his composure, James spotted a silver tray with a green smoothie sitting on the bed, untouched. Next to the smoothie was a carbon copy receipt bearing Laurence's signature, the date, and the time. According to the receipt, the drink was ordered or perhaps delivered around four thirty that afternoon. So, Gordon might have been the last person to see Laurence alive. James whirled around, then he crouched and gazed at Laurence. There didn't seem to be any evidence of tears on his cheeks or a note near the body. And there was something odd about the bullet wound, but he couldn't put his finger on it. As he stood, James spotted a bullet wedged in the door at his eye level.

So Laurence was facing the window when he died, and the bullet passed straight through his head, leaving gunpowder residue on the entry wound. James continued to gaze at the bullet. Laurence didn't shoot himself. Not that James was an expert, but if Laurence had shot himself, the bullet should have had an elevated angle, whereas that bullet appeared to be wedged into the door at an angle with a slight depression. Perhaps that meant that the murder was staged to appear as a suicide. Or maybe James was wrong about the angle of the bullet. And obviously, the recently deceased didn't put away or hide a gun.

James placed two fingers on the side of Laurence's neck. As he felt around for a pulse, he noticed that Laurence's hands lay palms down on the carpet and were free of blood and gunpowder residue. A minute passed, and James couldn't detect a pulse. There was no gun. On top of that, rigor mortis had already set in on most of his body. *So, Laurence died six hours ago, placing his murder around five p.m.*

That was definitely not a suicide, which meant whoever murdered Laurence had somehow left with the gun. Then James realised that if the killer had left the room via the door, they would have needed to lock it on the outside. Standing, James surveyed the room. The key didn't appear to be anywhere visible.

Careful not to disturb any evidence, James wandered over to the floor-to-ceiling writing bureau. He paused as he gazed at the droplets of blood splattered across the timber. Against his better judgement, he touched one droplet—the blood was dry. And the blood on the writing desk clearly hadn't been disturbed since the events had taken place. Dry blood also meant that Laurence had been there for some time.

James pulled down the handle of the bureau. Inside the desk was a small square key holder, wallet, notepad, an expensive-looking pen, and the room key. With the room key present, the murderer had to have left by another means.

Merde. How would he explain his tinkering with the crime scene to the local police? They were going to be suspicious of his behaviour. He needed to figure out who'd killed Laurence before the police blamed him. *Is the killer still in the bed-and-breakfast? Can I investigate Laurence's murder without painting a target on my back? And who would do this to Laurence?* Yes, the man was angry and difficult, but he didn't deserve such an end.

James wandered around the sea of evidence and slipped out of the room. Standing in the hallway, James glanced at Xavier and nodded towards the stairs. Xavier held up his finger, turned and locked the door, and followed him.

TEN

SATURDAY: 11:26 P.M.

AFTER JAMES RECOUNTED his findings and conclusions about the events that took place in Laurence's room, Xavier got up and pottered around the library. The elderly man picked up a rotary phone then trekked to his armchair with the phone line trailing him. Nestled in a Victorian-style armchair across from a series of floor-to-ceiling dark-stained bookshelves crammed with leather-bound books, James watched Xavier dial the rotary phone. The elderly man grimaced, pulled the receiver away from his ear, hung up, and redialled the number. Xavier repeated the ritual several times. James got up and wandered around the room, following the phone line. Nothing appeared to be out of the ordinary. So, the phone lines were down because of the storm.

Xavier sighed. 'The phone lines are down, the driveway to the property is flooded, and so is the town.'

James nodded as he surveyed the room. 'So we can't call the police.'

Xavier raised his eyebrows.

'Are you sure this is a safe place to talk?' James headed to the chair and sat.

'Yes. The stairs to the library hall creak, so we can hear anyone coming down. And the hinges on the door to the entrance hall creak as well. That's why we had it open during the day.'

'What about other entrances?'

'There's no other way to access the library without leaving the house and braving the weather.' Xavier glanced out the window at the rain. It fell on the window at a forty-five-degree angle.

The lights in the cast-iron chandelier flickered then brightened. A strong wind howled, and lightning shot across the sky, illuminating the front lawn. A cool breeze drifted out of the grey marble fireplace behind them.

'Do you think the killer is still in the bed-and-breakfast?' James brushed his hand along the fabric of the armchair.

'Yes, I suspect so.'

James cocked his head and squinted. As he'd aged, his vision had become blurry. Just like his grandfather, James had developed an astigmatism. As a result, he needed to wear his glasses. 'How do you know? You can't be certain.'

Xavier nodded. 'Yes, I can. We had no deliveries today. And no one had visitors.'

James shrugged. 'Just because you didn't see anyone doesn't mean someone didn't arrive and leave without you knowing.'

Xavier leaned back in his chair and chuckled. 'I locked the gate after Sybil and Honey arrived. Anyone who arrived after that had to press the buzzer to be let inside the grounds. The pedestrian gate is broken and cannot be opened. There's no way someone scaled the wall of the property. And how did they enter Laurence's room?'

Typical Xavier and his ironclad logic—poking holes in my conspiracy theory.

James pursed his lips as he examined the possibilities, staring at the blur of beige that resembled the drapes framing the giant four-panelled window. 'Maybe Laurence let them in.'

Xavier grumbled. 'Laurence is a Black man. Life has taught him to be cautious and cynical. He's experienced more than his fair share of harassment and ignorance. There's no way he let someone into his room and locked the door after the guest arrived. Let's face it. If that were to have happened, the guest would have retrieved the key and left the room, locking it behind them as they left.'

'Yeah, sorry. I completely overlooked that.' James closed his eyes and massaged the skin between his eyebrows. 'We need to figure out which one of the guests killed Laurence and stop them from leaving before the police arrive. And without arousing suspicion.'

'Hmm,' Xavier murmured.

'We could lead people to believe that we think he killed himself and try to figure out what was going on with him so we can tell his family what happened,' James said as he stared at the bookshelves.

Xavier nodded. 'I think that would work. I've met his wife a few times, so people should believe it.'

'And—' James raised his finger as a loud creak broke the silence of the house. He froze.

'The door,' Xavier whispered.

Someone was listening in on their conversation, but who? And could they be sure the sound came from the door leading to the entrance and the back east wing of the house and not the stairs?

'What about the stairs in the back east wing? Do they creak?'

Xavier shook his head.

'Who's staying in that wing?'

'Christopher Page and that Stella woman.' Xavier waved dismissively.

'And you're sure the creak isn't from the library staircase.'

Xavier shrugged and pointed at the ceiling. 'I believe we would have heard the patter of feet from above.'

An uneasy feeling swept over James as he stood and sauntered across the room. After opening the library door, he peered out into the empty hall. He could see the stairs without sticking his head out of the room. He pulled his smartphone from his pocket, opened the camera app, and used it as a mirror to see up the grand staircase, just like his girlfriend, Valentine, did when she needed to touch up her makeup. He, however, was trying to catch a killer. It was just as he expected—no one was there.

He scanned the hall. To his right was the entrance hall door. It, too, was closed. Someone had entered the hall without getting caught, but they'd screwed up on the way out. Either that or he was paranoid, like a teenage girl who had just watched her very first scary flick. His money was on the latter.

———

ELEVEN

TOGETHER, Xavier and James ascended the stairs and retired to their rooms for the rest of the evening. As James passed by Laurence's door, he wished he had laid a blanket over him and closed his eyes. But he was too busy figuring out what had happened and finding an excuse to investigate his murder to give Laurence that dignity. Sure, he was a jerk, but James felt bad for him. The man had probably looked into the eyes of his killer as they pulled the trigger. Was he terrified? Did he know why they wanted to kill him? And where was the gun?

At six minutes to midnight, James turned his doorknob and pushed open the door. Before him, a sea of items was scattered from one end of the room to the other—that was not how he'd left the room. His small wheeled suitcase was flung open in the middle of the floor, and the contents of his small carryall were spilling out through the open zipper. The bedsheets and duvet hung off the edge of the bed. Pillows were scattered across the carpet, not neatly stacked on the box seat under the window. The bed-and-breakfast's in-room pamphlets and miniature toiletries had been removed from the shelves in the wardrobe and thrown across the carpet. Based on the trail of scattered toiletries, it appeared that someone had opened the door, thrown the items over their shoulder, then moved on to the next thing on their ransacking to-do list. At least they didn't empty the liquids onto the carpet. Then James realised that, like an idiot, he'd left his door unlocked.

Someone had been busy. They had eavesdropped on his conversation with Xavier then ransacked his room. Or maybe it was the other way around. James sighed as he considered cleaning up before going to bed.

So that was what he did—he started cleaning. A few minutes later, James trekked to the door, fumbled around on the wall, and switched on the light. He gasped. Stabbed to the wardrobe with a letter opener was a sheet of paper bearing the bed-and-breakfast logo. It contained three simple words. It read:

Let it go.

The message was to the point, but it said so much more than it appeared. James was sure someone had listened to his conversation with Xavier. And it was someone who didn't want to kill him straightaway.

Why leave a threat when you can wait and finish someone off?

As he stared at the closed wardrobe door, a rock formed in the pit of his stomach. The door to the wardrobe had been closed. But he didn't remember closing it when he pulled out the robe and put it on before leaving the room and investigating the smell.

James inched towards the wardrobe with a sense of panic building within. His heart raced as he reached the closed doors. *What a stupid idea.* He should've left the room straightaway. But he was about to find out whether someone was lurking in the closet. He tugged on the small handles. The polished timber door creaked in protest. A lone hanger jiggled around on the rail. It was empty—there was no one inside. Crouching, he glanced under the bed. Yep, he was a moron. All he seemed to do was panic, jump to conclusions, and think later.

Leaving the note where he found it, he cleaned up his room and went to bed. As he lay his head on the pillow, James realised he had screwed up. He shouldn't have cleaned up. The police needed to see the room as he'd found it. Otherwise, it would seem like too much of a coincidence. *Merde.*

As he drifted to sleep, James wondered whether he should've told Xavier about what had happened to his room. He also wondered whether Xavier would be safe in his room with Flora.

TWELVE

SUNDAY: 9:11 A.M.

THE FOLLOWING DAY, James opted to eat breakfast in his room alone. After his discussion with Xavier then the ransacking of his room, he didn't fancy eating breakfast with a killer or listening to Sybil's bellyaching about the food she was served. James wanted to give that a hard pass. As he waited for room service to deliver his croissant and espresso, he sat on the box seat and stared out the window. He watched the rain beat down as the wind howled. Muffled chatter came from downstairs. Every now and then, James heard his name mentioned but not Laurence's, which was unusual. He expected Laurence's name to be on everyone's lips. A gentle knock at the door broke his train of thought.

James tugged at the white business shirt under his grey-heather polyester-knit jumper as he got up and strolled to the door. Upon opening it, he was greeted by Flora's warm smile and a tray with his breakfast.

'Oh my,' she said with a gasp.

He followed her gaze across the room to the note stabbed into the wardrobe door.

James shrugged. 'I kept it up for the police.'

Stepping aside, James opened the door a little wider, leaving room for Flora to enter. With her eyes fixed on the note, she carried the tray to the box seat and placed it down. Then she walked over to the message, tilted her head, and stared.

He closed the door and cleared his throat. 'You know, I was thinking of waiting to see if the cretin who wrote that would be stupid enough to sign the guest book, and if so, I could attempt to do a handwriting match.'

Flora glanced over her shoulder. 'That's an interesting thought. But what if they don't sign the guest book?'

James strolled across the room and sat on the edge of the box seat. 'That's suspicious, too, in a way. Why avoid signing the guest book for a new bed-and-breakfast? You'll be the first, and every guest will read your note.'

'Not everyone likes to write.' Flora ambled to the box seat and sat on the other side of the tray. 'Some people might struggle to formulate the right words and avoid it altogether.'

'I think Xavier has rubbed off on you.'

Flora shrugged. 'It's been over thirty years. So it was bound to happen, eventually.'

James nodded. 'During our walk yesterday

afternoon, you mentioned Xavier invited Laurence, and I gather you invited Stella. I was wondering who invited the other guests.'

'Hmm.' Flora leaned back and gazed out the window. 'Well, Stella recommended Sybil, who came with Honey. And Christopher Page was a guest of Laurence. Apparently, Laurence was a consultant on his upcoming film. The film is between shoots at the moment. They were supposed to travel to Morocco next week for more filming.'

'And Xavier invited me.'

'Dr Manesh Warren was supposed to attend, but he came down with a virus and thought it would be best to stay home.' Flora sighed.

'So, Stella knows Sybil and Honey.' James picked up the espresso and took a sip.

'Oh no, Sybil is a client at the PR firm Stella works for in Los Angeles.' Flora grimaced as she gazed out the window.

James pulled out his phone and typed a brief note into an app.

'Are you writing a story?' Flora had a hint of hesitation in her voice.

He paused. 'Oh no. I'm just investigating because I'm worried the police will like me for the murder. And I'm curious. Who did this?' James gestured to the note pinned to his wardrobe door.

'Sorry. It was rude of me to accuse you like that.' Flora got up off the box seat and brushed her hand along her floral blouse as she waltzed to the door.

'It's okay. I get why you would be worried about that.'

Flora paused in the middle of the room. 'I probably shouldn't be saying this, but I saw Laurence leave the cleaner's closet, and looking a little dishevelled, just after four. I can't be certain of the time.'

'And you didn't see who he was with?'

Flora walked to the door then twisted the brass knob. 'No.'

James nodded as Flora left the room and closed the door behind her, leaving him alone with his thoughts —and the smell, which seemed to have improved overnight.

So, only Christopher had a known affiliation with Laurence before attending the bed-and-breakfast. But then there was the mysterious argument between Stella and Laurence that happened close to midday. Was it a lover's quarrel like Flora thought, or was Laurence just wound up and picking a fight over something trivial?

James's eyes bulged—*the receipt*. He needed to confirm the time on the receipt and see whether anyone was in the room with Laurence at the time of the room service delivery. But before James spoke to anyone, he needed to write a few more thoughts about the discovery of Laurence's body, his conversation with Xavier, and the ransacking of his room.

———

STANDING OUTSIDE THE CLOSED DOOR, James listened to Gordon barking orders—and a familiar mumbled response. Wanting to avoid running into other guests, James slid open the door to the kitchen and stepped inside.

A mediaeval-style chandelier fitted with flame-shaped lightbulbs hung over the kitchen island in the centre of the room. Stacked on the island counter was a pile of dirty dishes containing partially eaten food and leftover sauce from breakfast. Off to the side, on top of a bench under a large window, was a row of three red-and-white-checked cushions bearing a neatly folded stack of tea towels. Curtains fastened with a cuff made of the same fabric framed the large window. The kitchen's country decor was quite surprising since the style didn't seem to suit Flora or Xavier. Perhaps their daughter, Rosaline, had decorated the kitchen.

'No guests allowed,' Gordon grumbled as he waved a spatula in his left hand. The man's knuckles were almost white.

Xavier nodded at James. 'It's okay. Just ignore him.'

'Hey,' Gordon moaned. 'I'm the head chef, and this is my kitchen.' Gordon pointed at him. 'And you can get out.'

James shrugged. 'Or I can help by clearing away these dirty dishes.'

'Hmm.' Gordon turned around and hovered over the silver saucepan on the black dual-range cooker.

The smell of the eggs caused James to salivate. And

like a rat following the tune of the pied piper, James strolled across the large white marble kitchen tiles to the black oven. Leaning against the white timber counter with black cast-iron handles, James breathed in the aroma. It smelt divine. But he had already eaten breakfast and was regretting his Parisian-style food. *What's happening to me?*

James sniffed. 'Smells good.'

Gordon groaned. 'Maybe you could share that with Lady Muck out there. This is the third time I've cooked this poached egg for her. There's nothing wrong with the eggs. I picked them up from a local supplier yesterday morning.'

James nodded and stepped back. 'So, it's just Sybil who sends food back. Right? It's not everyone. The other guests are perfectly pleasant.'

Gordon turned around and pointed the spatula at the ceiling. 'No, they're not.'

James raised his eyebrows.

'That imbecile from yesterday, yelling about Wi-Fi, gave me step-by-step instructions on how to make a green smoothie.' Gordon shook his head.

James exhaled. 'You haven't heard?'

Gordon lifted the lid of the saucepan. 'I don't have time for gossip. Get back to the dishes.'

'Laurence died last night. He shot himself in his room.'

Gordon narrowed his eyes. 'You mean someone didn't beat him to it?'

James walked to the island, picked up a plate off

the light-grey granite-top counter, strolled to the bin, scraped the food into the compost portion, and placed it into the sink. He glanced across the room at Gordon, who was busy preparing Sybil's poached egg. There was no love lost between Gordon and Laurence.

'I found his body,' James volunteered. 'He didn't touch the green smoothie. It looked nice.'

Gordon slammed the plate down on the edge of the kitchen island. 'I didn't poison him, if that's what you're implying.'

'No, I was wondering how he was behaving before he died. It seemed so out of the blue.' James trekked to the island and grabbed another plate.

Gordon nodded as he leaned against the kitchen island. 'Well, I delivered the smoothie around quarter to five. Knocked on the door. Laurence groaned then opened the door. He seemed annoyed that I was present.'

'So he was alone? Did he seem sad to you?'

Gordon tapped the counter. 'For a brief moment, I would've sworn I heard another voice. Nothing audible, just a faint whisper. When I opened the door, he was by himself. Cheesed off but not sad.'

'What happened after that? Did you see him again?'

Gordon narrowed his eyes. 'What's it to you?'

James rolled his eyes. 'Well, his family is going to be asking Xavier a lot of questions, and I just want to help him figure out what happened.'

'I see your point.' Gordon shrugged. 'He locked

the door, which was odd, and I went downstairs to fix Lady Muck her afternoon tea.'

Where is my afternoon tea? Everyone else was getting snacks while he was in the pool, starving.

'I bet that was a chore.'

'Nah, they were late, and Honey looked upset.' Gordon waved his hand dismissively. 'Who would blame her? She works for the Wicked Witch of the West.'

'Was this afternoon tea for everyone?'

'No.' Gordon waved his hand at James. 'Sybil demanded afternoon tea at quarter to five but didn't show until just after five. It was in the dining room. It wasn't a part of the bed-and-breakfast package.'

For the next fifteen minutes, James helped clear away dishes as he contemplated Gordon's words. So Laurence had a guest—potentially. *Did they hide when Gordon delivered the smoothie? Was that the reason Laurence was annoyed?* Honey's words echoed through his mind as he mulled over the possibilities. Yes, Laurence was married and had a lover—that made sense. Both Flora and Honey saw him leaving the cleaner's closet while looking dishevelled. So that must be correct. Two people wouldn't lie about the same thing. That would be ridiculous.

THIRTEEN

SUNDAY: 10:33 A.M.

AFTER SPENDING an hour drudging away in the kitchen as Gordon's errand boy, James finally escaped with the help of Xavier, who offered himself up as tribute to the merciless kitchen god. *Poor Xavier.* James felt terrible, but he needed to figure out who the killer was before he or Xavier became their next target.

As he strolled up the corridor towards the closed door to the entrance hall, a solution to his next problem came to mind. Smiling, James dashed to the closed door. Asking questions without rousing suspicion wasn't going to be easy, but he had thought of the perfect angle with which to approach Sybil without hinting that he suspected foul play. He would appeal to her ego. That should be the ideal distraction.

He tugged on the iron handle, pulled the heavy door to him, and stepped into the entrance hall. Hunched over the large round table in the centre of the room, Christopher was writing in the guest book. A startled look swept across his face, and he jumped back. After he regained his composure, Christopher's expression transformed into a glare. It was almost as if the man was given a cue and his demeanour changed.

Christopher furrowed his brow. 'I don't recall seeing you at breakfast.'

James rolled his eyes.

The man's eyes widened. 'We have a killer roaming around the halls of this house.' Christopher's eyes darted to the window that overlooked the front garden. 'And you not being at breakfast was suspicious.'

So, that's what they were chatting about over breakfast. They were forming a conspiracy theory club.

James shrugged. 'Save your conspiracy theories for someone else. Laurence ended his life. It's tragic, but that's what the evidence suggests.'

Christopher stalked across the room to James. 'The day Laurence died, he was angry and infuriating to be around, but I don't believe he was secretly depressed. Laurence loved every second of his involvement in my film. And Laurence was pedantic about insignificant details and enjoyed making decisions that affected many of the set's visual aspects and even the plot. He was looking forward to the next stage of filming. In his own weird way, he was somewhat happy.' Christopher towered over James. 'And happy people don't kill themselves.'

James shook his head. 'What's this to do with me not being at breakfast?'

'Yesterday, I heard you picking a fight with Laurence when you arrived.' Christopher glanced towards the large front window. 'He was rude to your grandfather, so you grabbed Sybil's gun and shot him.'

So, he knows about Sybil's missing gun. Did he just incriminate himself, or did Sybil blab to everyone around the breakfast table? As much as he would love to see Christopher dragged away from Clovervale Hall in handcuffs, James knew there was only one logical reason for Christopher's newfound knowledge— cyclone Sybil and her big mouth. *And why am I allowing this man to get under my skin? Is this just cabin fever?*

James took a step back then trekked around Christopher and across the room to the closed door leading to the library hall. He paused. 'Xavier was one of my old college professors,' James said over his shoulder. 'And why would I murder Laurence over his squabble with Xavier? In that scenario, he's more likely to end up with a black eye in the event that I could actually be bothered to hit him.' James whirled around. 'But I rarely get that worked up over someone. So, as I asked, what does this have to do with me not turning up for breakfast?'

The room fell silent as Christopher grimaced and surveyed the room.

'It has nothing to do with me eating alone. You're

spinning a web of conspiracy and haven't thought things through. The worst thing you can do right now is create more panic and drama.' James slipped his hands into his pockets, strolled across the room to the antique reception table, and plucked a map from the small stand on the desk.

As he passed by the round table on his second trip to the library hall, he spotted Christopher's signature on the guest book. The vain cretin had left his autograph, not a message about how he'd enjoyed the bed-and-breakfast or a thank-you message for the hosts. Instead, he'd made it all about himself.

James stared up into Christopher's cerulean-blue eyes. 'If you must know, I ate breakfast alone in my room because I couldn't bear to spend another second with your vain arse or that of the other drama queens who stalk these halls.'

James stalked across the room and to the door. For the first time, he had the burning desire to punch someone. Besides James's newfound thirst for violence, the second most fascinating thing was that James wasn't the only one who didn't buy Laurence's staged murder. Laurence was certainly not in the headspace where he would have contemplated ending his life.

After grabbing the handle, James pulled the door open. The hinges moved under the strain of the heavy door and let out a familiar squeak. James let the door close behind him. A sea of thoughts swirled in his mind. Perhaps he was reaching new depths of cynicism, but he couldn't help but feel as if someone was attempting to ruin his reputation. And if so, did Christopher reach those conclusions all by himself, or was someone else lurking behind the scenes, helping him build his conspiracy theory?

———

AFTER NINETEEN MINUTES of writing notes and mentally rehearsing his subtle attempt at questioning Sybil, with his heart racing, James took several deep breaths before knocking on the door of room four. As he mulled over the questions in his mind, he heard the smooth jazz come to an abrupt halt as feet shuffled across the floor. Thunder crackled, and the rain continued to beat down on the small window in the hall outside the room.

The door flung open. Standing before him was Sybil in what appeared to be workout gear—black leggings, a tight black T-shirt with sweat-resistant material, bright-pink trainers, and a matching bright-pink hand towel.

Sybil stared up into James's blue-green eyes with a look of determination. 'Well, where is it?'

'What?' James stepped back.

Sybil sighed. 'Annie, you dimwit.'

Her eyes darted down the hall as if she was checking to be sure no one was listening to their conversation. She grasped his left bicep with her right hand, dragged him into the room, and slammed the door behind them. Room four looked similar in layout to his and Laurence's with a few exceptions. The decor included a beige floral material and a fireplace, and a timber door in the top left-hand corner of the room led to an en suite bathroom. *It turns out that if you act like an unbearable diva, you get the best room.*

'Well,' Sybil demanded, breaking his train of thought.

So, it's all about the gun for her. No concern about Laurence, just Annie. Interesting.

James sighed. 'I didn't get a good look around Laurence's room.'

Sybil slapped him with her hand towel. 'Rubbish. You were in that room forever.'

James shrugged. 'It didn't feel that way to me. I checked his pulse and looked around the room to confirm that it was indeed a suicide and no foul play was at hand.'

'Well,' Sybil whispered as she leaned in conspiratorially.

'There was no note. He just...'

'Annie? What about my Annie? I know he offed himself. That's obvious,' she said in a dismissive tone.

James bit the inside of his lip. 'I can't alter the scene or share any more details than that. Otherwise, when the police get here, they might consider you knowing something about the scene to be suspicious. And I'm sure you don't want that.'

Sybil hung her head. 'I suppose.'

James narrowed his eyes. *Should I even ask? What's the worst that could happen?*

'Sybil.' James hesitated. 'Is Annie registered with the police?'

Her head sprang to attention. 'Of course,' Sybil replied. 'Don't be daft.' She rubbed her neck.

The two stood in silence and stared at the fireplace along the wall separating their rooms.

James cleared his throat as he ambled over to the box seat under the large window and sat. 'Gordon mentioned at dinner last night that you're a food blogger.'

Sybil followed him across the room and took a seat. 'That man is an utter nightmare, and he's so unprofessional. I've worked in the restaurant industry for two decades, and Gordon is the worst. He was fired from a five-star restaurant in New York City, you know.' Sybil straightened her posture as she glanced at James.

So, she can tell when other people are acting out. Interesting.

'Yes, he was kind of rude.' James leaned forwards and stared at the floor to regain his composure and avoid laughing. 'Like you'—he glanced over at Sybil— 'I'm writing a piece on Xavier's bed-and-breakfast and was wondering when you plan to publish your review. Since you're probably reviewing the cuisine, I could mention your post in the *Northampton Tribune*. It would interest the newspaper readers.'

Sybil's eyes sparkled. 'Oh, that would be wonderful. Honey nagged me to death to visit this technology-free bed-and-breakfast, and I honestly thought it would be a complete waste of my time. I relented anyway and thought it was a huge mistake, but I'm so glad I did.'

She jumped up from the box seat then dashed across the room to the writing bureau, opened it, and pulled out a black leather folio-style planner with coloured tabs along the side. Cradling the large diary in her arms, she opened it and flicked through the pages. Sybil paused. With her index finger, she scanned the page and froze for a few seconds.

'Six p.m. Eastern Standard Time on Monday, the twenty-first of April, is when my post will be released.' Sybil gazed up from the diary. 'I've already started writing it, you know.'

James nodded as Sybil slammed the diary shut, returned it to the writing bureau, then trekked across the room. Thunder crackled far off in the distance, and the wind howled, shaking the window.

'I'm happy to write a fair and honest review for your paper. Something short to include with your article, maybe a twenty-word teaser. The first one is free,' Sybil said with a slight smile.

Wow. She's almost pleasant to be around.

James nodded. 'I'll have to talk to the owner and the board of the paper before I engage your services, even if they're free.'

Sybil cocked her head. 'I thought you would have more control than that as the chief editor.'

James sighed. 'Let's not discuss the politics and bureaucracy of my job. It's a real mood killer. You mentioned Honey nagged you to do this. How did she find out about it? You're both from America. It's a long way to travel for a B and B opening.'

'Actually, that's not entirely true. I was born here and went to school in Yorkshire then left to study in the US and never returned. But Honey is my personal assistant, and she regularly searches for openings of new places for me to critique. So, I guess the internet was where she found out about the opening.' Sybil rubbed her neck.

'How is Honey doing? Someone mentioned to me that she was upset yesterday afternoon.'

Sybil narrowed her eyes. 'Why ask me?'

James leaned back as he sensed hostility in Sybil's tone. 'I thought it might make her uncomfortable if I enquired about her well-being. I wouldn't want her to get the wrong idea.'

Sybil's expression softened. 'It was just PMS. You're a man. You'll never understand what it's like.'

An uncomfortable silence swept over the room. As the seconds ticked by, James realised that he had the perfect excuse to make a run for it. He would have to think of another way to approach Sybil and ask her more questions at a later stage. Then, he realised there was no point beating about the bush—it would be far less painful to simply ask her about Laurence. There was no point in torturing himself twice; a second conversation might seem suspicious.

Rising from his seat, he strolled across the room then paused. 'Sybil, when did you last see Laurence?

How did he appear to you? It's just occurred to me that his family is going to ask Xavier a lot of questions, and I think it would be nice if he could give them some answers.'

James whirled around as Sybil murmured to herself.

'Maybe I saw him last around quarter to five in the evening, before our afternoon tea. He was sneaking into the library.'

James narrowed his eyes. *That can't be right. I was coming back from the pool at that time. I would've seen him.*

'Are you sure it was a quarter to five?'

Sybil groaned. 'Or maybe it was earlier than that. I can't be certain of the time, but I saw him leave the library.'

James nodded. 'So he was leaving the library?'

'That's what I said,' Sybil snapped as she rubbed her neck.

Oh, no you didn't.

James continued to nod. 'How did he seem?'

'Annoyed, maybe bitter, and a little sad.' Sybil nodded. 'Yes, his eyes seemed sad.' She sighed. 'But mostly angry. He was a very angry man.'

After exchanging a polite smile with Sybil, James sauntered to the door, left, and closed it behind him. Not only did Sybil's story have huge holes, but she was also a terrible liar and had an obvious tell. *But why lie about seeing Laurence in the library? Is she covering up something? Or is she just trying to appear as if she knows something and thus be valuable somehow? And where did her hostility about Honey's well-being come from?*

The more questions he asked, the more questions arose. But there was one thing that he was certain about. He was going to have to talk to Honey.

FOURTEEN

THE FLOORBOARDS CREAKED as James headed down the corridor and followed the hall to the right. As he passed the wall separating the back east wing from the front east wing, James couldn't hear a sound. It was almost eerie. *Where are Stella and Christopher?*

He paused outside of room seven. A faint lavender fragrance floated past his nose as he listened to the rhythmic tapping. It sounded like typing. *Does Honey have a blog as well?* It made sense. Perhaps she was just starting out and was working with Sybil until her blog made more money. A blogger could work for years before they generated an audience large enough to make a sizeable income, or so he had read in an article he had edited for the *Northampton Tribune*.

The pattering of the keys continued nonstop for another two minutes. After feeling like a creep for eavesdropping, James knocked on the door. The tapping abruptly halted, then a series of thumps followed. A few seconds later, a drawer slammed shut, and the room was quiet. *So, she's doing some secret blogging. Why keep it a secret?* Then he realised. *Sybil doesn't know about Honey's secret project. Now that's interesting.*

Five minutes later, the door opened.

Honey popped her head between the gap and smiled. 'OMG, I didn't hear you. I was in a world of my own, flipping through pages of *InStyle*—it's a fashion magazine. You know how it is.'

James raised his eyebrows. *Is that intended as a subtle hint? Or is she just a terrible liar?*

She pulled the door back, allowing him to enter. With a flick of her long, straight black hair, Honey waltzed across the room and sat at the edge of her four-poster bed.

Wanting to avoid any awkward conversations with Valentine when he got home, James strolled across the room and sat on the box seat under the window, which was perfectly positioned between a pair of open yellow-and-green vine-print curtains. James peered out at the driveway and the front facade of Clovervale Hall. From Honey's room, he could see Laurence's window, but the heavy rain pelting against the glass made it difficult to see anything beyond that.

'It's raining pretty hard out there,' Honey said as she sat on the bed and looked out the window at the front lawn.

'Hmm,' James murmured. 'I was just thinking

about Laurence. I feel bad. It happened right under my nose, and I didn't even notice he was so depressed.'

Honey rose from the bed, strolled across the room, and sat next to him. She sighed. 'Some people hide their depression well. My adoptive mother was excellent at hiding things. Her passing came as a shock.' Honey's eyes glazed over.

James nodded. 'Sorry. I didn't realise this would be quite triggering for you.'

She sniffled. 'I'm fine.' Honey waved her hand dismissively. 'It happened when I was just out of high school. It was a long time ago.' Her voice trailed off and seemed full of regret.

'Was that why you were upset yesterday afternoon? Xavier was a little concerned and mentioned it to me,' James lied.

Honey's posture stiffened as she leaned away from him. *Merde—I've spooked her.*

James shrugged. 'Don't worry. He was just panicking about everything that was going wrong during the opening. He was my former university professor. We go way back.'

'Oh.' Honey let out a deep breath. 'No, I'm just a little sensitive and overreacted to Laurence snapping at me.'

'Just before your afternoon tea with Sybil?'

Honey narrowed her eyes at James. 'Y-yes.' A hint of hesitation in her voice.

James sighed. 'Why is everyone getting fancy afternoon teas?'

'Sybil demanded one from the chef.' She leaned in and whispered, 'He was super cheesed, and she gave him no other instructions. It was as if she expected him to read her mind or just know.' Honey chuckled.

'Maybe Laurence was hangry. That's a thing, apparently.' James nodded. 'My grandmother went on a diet to lose five kilograms. Don't ask from where because my grandfather and I are still trying to figure that out. Let's just say it was the worst two weeks of our lives.'

Honey smiled briefly. 'Actually, I knocked on his door and invited him to our afternoon tea. That's when he tore me a new one.'

'Maybe he had a guest in his room. From the cleaner's closet.' James raised his eyebrows.

Honey's mouth dropped open as she pointed at the bed. 'For the briefest of moments, I swear, I heard a second voice just before I knocked, and then the room went quiet.' She nodded. 'I didn't see anyone when he opened the door, not that you can call it opening the door. It was barely ajar, and all I could see were his eyes.'

'So, you didn't see who was with him in the closet?'

Honey tilted her head and looked all doe-eyed at him. 'Are you accusing me of lying?'

A bolt of lightning flashed across the sky, and James jumped. Seconds later, the dark-grey sky erupted with an explosion of thunder.

'No, but I'm curious.' James clutched his chest as

he looked at the storming skies. 'Don't you want to know who was in there with Laurence? It's not exactly romantic.'

Honey bit her lip. 'I don't know about that. I think it's super romantic. Imagine going at it with someone in the cleaner's closet, knowing that if anyone comes up the stairs, they'll be able to hear you. I would definitely go at it in that closet with Christopher. He's so much more than a dish. He's practically a three-course meal.'

James rolled his eyes. 'Yeah, until he opens his mouth.'

Honey burst out laughing. 'Someone's a little jealous.' She nudged him with her elbow. 'Or maybe you go both ways.'

James shook his head.

She shrugged her left shoulder. 'You're no fun.'

'You're talking about having sex in a cleaner's closet with that cretin.'

Honey wrinkled her nose. 'You shouldn't use that word. I'm not sure what it means in your native language, but in English, it's quite a derogatory term. It's offensive. And we've been through this. The cleaner's closet is super romantic. You're stealing a moment away with someone, no matter how brief.'

'Yeah, it's all super romantic until you get bleach or cleaning acid spilt on you. And Christopher has all of those tattoos. So he'll want to keep those harsh cleaning products away from them.'

'OMG, that's so grim.'

'And why go from the cleaner's closet to his bedroom? Why not just go straight to his room? It's more comfortable.' James furrowed his brow.

Honey giggled. 'Wow, I feel sorry for your girlfriend. Romance isn't about comfort or practicality. It's about spontaneity and excitement. Comfort is where romance dies.'

Now, that was an insult. I'm plenty romantic.

'Or maybe they went to the closet after,' James said, ignoring her statement.

'No, it was before.' Honey laughed. 'I saw him leave around four. I didn't want to hang around because he seemed enraged.'

James angled his head towards Honey. 'Sybil said she saw him leaving the library on the way to your afternoon tea.'

Honey screwed up her face. 'No, that was when we arrived. He stormed into the house, through the library hall, and slammed the door. We never saw him exit.'

James nodded. 'I think he had a stressed-out personality and got easily worked up about things.'

'Yeah.' Honey sighed.

The pair sat in silence and listened to the rain beat down on the window. Then after the longest and most awkward seven minutes of his life, James nudged Honey.

'How did you end up with an invitation to this bed-and-breakfast opening? Aren't you from America? It's a long way to go just for a long weekend.'

Honey shrugged. 'I'm not the only foreigner here.'

'I'm French. I grew up in central western France in a university city called Poitiers,' James said, hoping that divulging information would encourage her to do the same.

A puzzled expression swept across Honey's face. 'I meant that Xavier, Christopher, Gordon, and Laurence are the only Brits here. The rest are from elsewhere.'

'No, Sybil's a British ex-pat who lives in America. She's not American.'

Honey shrugged off James's comment. 'Sybil rarely shares personal information with me, so I didn't know that. I did, however, discover that she got divorced a couple of decades ago. So, just between you and me, Sybil Curry is a pen name.'

James's eyes widened. 'What's her real name?'

'I can't say. Sybil was furious when she caught me red-handed. I had a file open with a few details that I learned about her. Just in case someone dropped some tea to a gossip blog or in a forum. I wanted to be prepared for all eventualities. It's a good PR practice. But I dropped it in the end You know how it is. I don't want to poke the bear.'

James pursed his lips then sighed. 'So, you're her personal assistant?'

Honey nodded. 'Yeah, I do a truckload of things for her. I'm from Seattle, by the way, and Sybil lives in San Francisco.' She smiled politely. 'I wanted to do something different from restaurant openings and filming cooking segments on YouTube. So I found this cute bed-and-breakfast online because their website said that Gordon Morrison, the former head chef at the Frog and Snail in New York, was in charge of the kitchen.' Honey gestured towards the floor. 'I've always wanted to eat at his restaurant, but he was fired, and new staff were hired. The restaurant changed hands and the customers stopped going.'

'Do you think it could be Stella?'

'What?' Honey's eyes widened. 'In the cleaner's closet? Oh, gawd—they hate each other.'

James shrugged. 'You've never had sex with someone you hate?'

'OMG, you're such a gossip.'

'Everyone likes to gossip. It's human nature.'

Honey shook her head. 'You can cross Stella off your list. She's a boring, ambitious social climber.'

James raised his eyebrows. 'So, I'm not the only one who likes to gossip.'

'No, that one is one hundred percent true.' Honey tilted her head and glanced at James with her big brown eyes. 'Scouts honour.'

'It's still gossiping.' James stood and ambled to the door.

'Sybil is a client of Stella's PR firm. I know her well. Stella recommended me to Sybil's PR manager. My adopted mother is Stella's second cousin on her mother's side or something like that.' Honey blurted out from across the room, 'I had to ask her to recommend me after Xavier didn't reply to my emails.

I had to practically beg Stella to get me and Sybil invited.'

James chuckled as he continued to stroll to the door. 'Hey, I believe you.' He paused and turned. 'But I need to check up on Xavier. He's super stressed. Maybe I can help him find a rainy-day activity for us all.'

A mischievous expression swept across Honey's face. 'I can think of one for two.'

James blushed. 'I have a girlfriend.'

Then James opened the door and left the room. So, the mysterious person in the closet with Laurence was not Stella, if what Honey said was true. And technically, Honey had an interesting alibi that couldn't be corroborated easily. Then why hadn't Sybil mentioned inviting Laurence to afternoon tea? James headed down the hall, mulling over the newfound information from Honey. *But is she a reliable source?* It was time for him to chat with Stella and come up with a rainy-day activity with Xavier.

As James turned the corner, Michelangelo was perched on the windowsill, meowing towards Laurence's door. James wondered whether the cat had seen anything. *Don't be ridiculous. He's a cat and just wants to be petted and fed a second breakfast.*

FIFTEEN

EIGHT MINUTES LATER, James crept across the hall in the back east wing as he listened to Stella and Christopher chatting in the sitting room. The dark-pine, half-wall modular panelling skirted the hall and perfectly blended in with the door and the grand staircase. Much like the dining room, the back east wing felt like it had been built in a different period—added in more prosperous years during the life of the manor house. Nestled in the corner of the hall close to the staircase was a Victorian armchair upholstered in a brownish floral-patterned fabric that was probably supposed to be beige.

James paused, hoping his eavesdropping would go undiscovered. Christopher was making fun of Sybil, and his impression was good. Predictably, Stella giggled along at all the right places. *If only he kept his best acting performances for the silver screen.*

Now that he knew where they were, James

considered doing a bit of amateur espionage. The idea was too enticing. Before he could reason with himself and point out the multitude of things that could go wrong, James glided up the stairs and passed the two large windows that overlooked the grand staircase. *What an idiot.*

As he reached the top of the back east wing's staircase, the partially open door of room five came into view. He had hit the jackpot. Like the north-seeking poles in iron atoms, he shot across the landing, passed the shared bathroom, and stood inches away from the ajar door. He pushed it open.

To his surprise, the room before him was a sea of chaos. And that room hadn't been ransacked. Scattered across the lush, thick carpet was a mixture of men's and women's clothing. Upon closer inspection, the clothes appeared to be left where they'd been dropped. The duvet was missing. The bedsheets were half off the bed and cascaded onto the floor. That was unexpected, and he knew someone who would be more than a little disappointed by the discovery. *Poor, Honey. Stella got there first.*

Tiptoeing around the fashion obstacle course, James meandered over to the small wheeled suitcase. It was unzipped.

A French luxury-branded logo was subtly etched on the dark-brown checked canvas—beautifully crafted. He was a little jealous. James had always wanted to own a large trunk, one of those cases that the upper class used when they travelled on luxury cruise ships in the early 1900s. He brushed his fingers along the coated leather and flipped open the front flap.

Protruding out of the inside flap was a clear document wallet. It appeared to be a certificate of some kind. Through the clear but foggy plastic, James could see the edge of a pale-blue border and a hint of a gold-embossed stamp in the bottom left-hand corner. *Perhaps her firm has won an award.*

A hint of curiosity built within him. He leaned forwards and pulled out the certificate. James froze. *Oh, la vache.*

It was a wedding certificate issued in Nevada one week ago, and a familiar signature appeared under Stella's.

Suddenly, the argument in the hedge maze made sense. He wasn't witnessing a wound-up man picking a fight over something trivial but the collapse of a love triangle—one that he didn't see coming. Or maybe he was jumping to conclusions and performing a mental gymnastics routine worthy of a gold medal.

Upon second thought, maybe Laurence had hooked up with Stella in the cleaner's closet one last time, and Christopher had found out then paid Laurence a visit—one last visit. That was plausible. And Christopher didn't like to lose. He was even willing to cheat in a non-confrontational board game.

As James's mind continued to spin through the possibilities, he became aware that the east wing was silent. Stella and Christopher weren't laughing anymore. Maybe they'd left the sitting room.

James froze as he listened to a thumping sound that was drawing nearer. Someone was walking up the stairs.

In desperation, James threw the certificate back into the suitcase and shut it, then he crawled around and hid on the other side of the bed. With any luck, he could crawl into the wardrobe and simply disappear. As James reached the other side of the bed, he noticed the closet was on the opposite side of the room. He'd paid no attention to the room's layout when he started snooping. And he was going to pay the price for his laziness. Glancing under the bed, James spotted a pair of polished bespoke men's shoes. Christopher was standing in the doorframe. *Merde.*

SIXTEEN

SUNDAY: 11:49 A.M.

AFTER WHAT FELT like the longest minute of James's life, Christopher ambled away as if he had not a care in the world. The polished dark-pine door to the sitting room slammed shut. James's heart raced as he let out a breath that he was holding in. More snooping was out of the question. *But is it still wise to interview Stella and Christopher, even under the guise of seeking information for Laurence's loved ones?*

James wanted to do it for Xavier and to provide answers to the police when they arrived. And he couldn't expect Xavier to do it on his own. That seemed wrong.

After he waded through the sea of clothing, James tiptoed down the stairs, making no sound. As he reached the bottom of the stairs, hushed murmurs could be heard from within the sitting room. One of them sounded suspicious about something, but he couldn't quite make out what was being said.

While approaching the closed double doors, James ran through the questions he had for Stella. *Just ask then get the hell out of there.* That was all he had to do.

His chest tightened as he approached the closed door. Briefly, he gazed out the window. The furniture in the courtyard had been tossed aside by the violent winds as the rain continued to pelt down. It was chaos.

After taking another deep breath, James turned the handle and pushed the door open. As he entered and closed the door behind him, the room fell silent. Stella narrowed her eyes at James as she lounged on the large beige sofa with the rounded arms. To his left, Christopher leaned against the side of the open marble fireplace, clutching a wrought iron fire poker. With his cerulean-blue eyes, he peered at James. As the seconds ticked by, the stare became increasingly uncomfortable.

'You were just in my room,' Stella said from the sofa.

Christopher's head swivelled back to Stella, and his eyes widened.

'No,' James lied.

Stella groaned. 'I heard someone upstairs just a moment ago, and now you're conveniently here. That's suspicious.'

James ran his fingers through his thick dark-blond hair. 'It's an old house. The floors are bound to creak from time to time. It's perfectly normal.'

A warm hand rested on the small of his back. James froze.

'Ignore her. She's completely paranoid,' Christopher whispered, still clutching the poker.

James stepped back.

'I heard that.' Stella turned and glanced out the window. 'And I'm not paranoid. I heard footsteps.'

James raised his eyebrows. 'You sound so certain. What are you so worried about? Do you have dark secrets lurking undiscovered in your room?'

Christopher snorted.

'I know you were in my room.' Stella pointed at James. 'And, you just admitted it.'

'Stella.' Christopher laughed. 'He's merely winding you up. He's simply bored like the rest of us.' Christopher nudged James.

'Guilty.' James held his hands up in mock surrender.

Stella snarled at him. So she'd heard him, after all. Thankfully, she sent Christopher to do a half-hearted investigation and didn't go upstairs herself. *Why is she paranoid? Because of her Vegas wedding? Or is she hiding something more sinister upstairs, something I missed?*

Christopher stepped back, leaned against the open fireplace, and prodded the wood with the wrought iron poker.

'Christopher tells me you believe Laurence ended things last night,' Stella said with a lingering sadness. 'I can't believe he's gone,' she added as her voice broke into sobs.

The fire crackled as Christopher struck the log a

few more times, seemingly unmoved by his new wife's tears. James wondered why he wasn't comforting her. But maybe James was being too harsh with Christopher. The man could be trying to keep the marriage under wraps, away from public scrutiny, or perhaps he was just a self-absorbed jerk. *If it walks like a duck and quacks like a duck...*

James strolled across the room and sat on the large round ottoman between the two mismatched antique sofas. Reaching out, he grabbed Stella's hand.

'Did he leave a note?' Stella asked.

James squirmed in his seat. 'I shouldn't give out the details of what I found. When the police arrive, they might find your knowledge suspicious.'

She pulled her hand away and wiped her dry eyes. For the briefest of moments, Stella had James convinced she was actually crying. *She should give Christopher a few pointers.*

'Sorry, I don't have any tissues.' James patted the pockets of his jeans. 'Did you know him well?'

Stella paused and stared at him. A hint of scepticism lingered in the air. So James wasn't the only one seeking information.

James nodded as he considered his next words. 'I ask because I saw Laurence getting heated with you in the hedge maze yesterday. At the time, I thought he was continuing his tour of rage. I never realised you knew each other. That's all.'

'Oh, you saw that.' Stella pursed her lips.

'He also honked his horn at me and gave me the

middle finger while I was turning in to the driveway, then he tore Xavier a new one about the lack of Wi-Fi.'

Christopher snorted.

James glanced up. That man had no sense of decorum. He was talking about a recently deceased man, and Christopher was in the mood to laugh. Obviously, there was no love lost between Christopher and Laurence.

'The website said technology-free retreat.' Christopher shook his head.

'Why?' Stella asked in a harsh tone. 'What's it to you?'

James sighed. 'Who do you think will have to tell Laurence's family about his death?'

Stella's face softened. 'Okay. Why isn't Xavier asking me this?'

James rolled his eyes. 'Because he's in his seventies and has a heart condition. I'm helping him out.'

'Fine.' Stella glared at James. 'Promise you won't tell a soul.'

'You mean other than Xavier?' James raised his eyebrows.

'Yes, I know Laurence,' she confessed, ignoring his last question. 'We were lovers,' she said as her voice broke, right on cue. 'We were having an affair, and he wouldn't leave his wife, even though he promised me he would. A few weeks ago, we had a fight while I was visiting him on set. That's where I met Christopher,' she said through a sea of tears.

James nodded. 'And you were in the maze when you told Laurence about your new relationship?'

'Yes, that's right,' Christopher chimed in.

Glancing over his shoulder, James spotted Christopher standing a short distance behind him, clutching the wrought iron poker.

James nodded. 'Oh, you think he was emotionally distressed over the news and did something stupid?'

Stella bawled. 'It's all my fault.' Leaning over, Stella shielded her face from view as she continued to sob. Her body jerked as she cried.

Christopher sighed. 'I'm not so sure.'

James leaned back. 'I'm just trying to figure out what was going on with Laurence so Xavier can give the man's family some answers. And the evidence suggests one likely scenario. What the police and Xavier choose to tell them is out of my hands.'

Stella sat up. 'You think this is my fault?'

Inwardly, James sighed. He didn't know how long he could keep up the charade. And he couldn't decide whether he was being tested by Christopher or if he genuinely believed Laurence was happy before his death. The truth was, the man was anything but happy. He was full of rage, and it seeped out of him— the man could barely contain it.

'No, I don't think it's reasonable to blame anyone in these circumstances. I'm sorry I've upset you.' James rose from the ottoman. 'I should help Xavier plan a rainy-day activity for everyone. We can all use the distraction.' James ambled to the closed door.

Stella sniffed. 'You should talk to Sybil. She and Laurence were eyeing each other on one occasion. It seemed quite intense, if you ask me.'

James paused and sighed. 'You mean the scary lady who chose places for us at dinner?'

'The one and only.' Stella smirked.

'What's her deal?'

Stella shrugged. 'You didn't hear it from me, but her real name is Eleanor Norrison.'

James whirled around. 'No.'

Christopher gasped. 'She's related to Gordon?'

'Divorced,' Stella said in a sweet voice.

James shook his head. 'It doesn't surprise me that Laurence and Sybil were fighting. Thanks for the heads-up.' James trekked to the door and left then closed the door behind him. But before he got the chance to consider the new information and Stella's sudden change in demeanour, he was confronted by an unexpected sight.

SEVENTEEN

SUNDAY: 12:02 P.M.

STANDING in the hall and with his hands on his hips, Xavier wore a familiar disappointed expression. *Merde. I'm about to get in trouble for gossiping.* Xavier raised an eyebrow at James as he nodded towards the hall that led to the main section of Clovervale Hall. Xavier leaned forward, grabbed James by the arm, and dragged him out of the hall and down the corridor. His former professor had a surprisingly firm grip.

'You almost got caught snooping in Stella's room,' Xavier said over his shoulder as he continued to march, dragging him into the entrance hall.

James rolled his eyes. 'So, you were listening in the entire time.'

Xavier halted in the middle of the entrance hall. 'No, I hid in Christopher's room while you walked up the stairs. I thought you were Stella or Christopher.'

James bit the inside of his lower lip as he pictured Xavier searching the rooms in the back east wing.

He slapped James in the centre of his chest. 'What? You don't think I can snoop around like everyone else?'

'I never said that.'

'Yes, you did.' Xavier peered at James inquisitively. 'I could see it in your eyes. You were trying not to laugh.'

James sighed. 'Stella and Christopher married in Vegas about a week ago, and she confessed to having an affair with Laurence.'

'I know,' Xavier replied. 'Please don't tell me you believe all those pretty words about him leaving his wife for Stella. There's no way that woman believed that. She clung to him around the time he had that international book tour. Laurence was a rising star at one point, then he flamed out spectacularly.'

James smirked. *Look who's gossiping now.*

Xavier pointed at James. 'And thanks to you, I now have to stop snooping and organise a rainy-day activity.'

'Why don't you get your big-screen TV and the DVD player out? The ones I sent you as a gift for the opening.' James leaned against the large round table.

Xavier murmured, 'It's supposed to be a technology-free retreat.'

James shook his head. 'Yes, but if you give in and let everyone watch a film, you can go back to snooping.'

'You realise that I have a PhD and am quite capable

of joining the dots for myself.' Xavier peered over the rims of his spectacles.

James held his hands up in mock surrender. 'I'm just trying to help you embrace your newfound hobby.'

For the next few minutes, James filled Xavier in on everything he had learned through his interviews. As he continued relaying the facts, Xavier stared across the room, murmuring to himself. James turned. There was nothing behind him.

'What is it?'

Xavier looked up at him. 'What did she mean by saying Sybil and Laurence were eyeing each other? It's a strange thing to say.'

James furrowed his brow. 'I thought Stella suggested they were fighting and still reeling from a fight later in the day.'

'I suppose.' Xavier strolled to the closed entrance hall door and opened it.

The door squeaked in protest as Xavier turned around and raised an eyebrow at James. 'I was right,' he whispered.

On his way to the library hall, James wandered around the large round table and peered at the guest book. Spread across a single page was a short message written with neat but elegant penmanship. It read:

Beautiful gardens, exquisite food, and friendly staff. A haven away from the stresses of life.

Xavier cleared his throat. 'Hurry. You need to get something from the attic before lunch.'

EIGHTEEN

SUNDAY: 12:27 P.M.

WHILE EVERYONE WAS SITTING in the exquisite dining room, eating a beef stew that was remarkably similar to beef bourguignon, James followed Xavier up the hall in the front east wing of Clovervale Hall. The elderly man clutched a long metal rod with a hook. That should have been James's first clue that he was in for a wild afternoon.

Standing on the landing near the bathroom and loo between Sybil and Honey's rooms, Xavier held the pole in his left hand, inched it towards the tiny hole in the ceiling, and pulled. A hatch flew down, and a set of narrow stairs unravelled into the hallway.

With an audience comprising an elderly man in his seventies and a grey feline who was suspiciously quiet, James spent half an hour dragging the LCD TV along the attic floor and turning it at different angles before successfully pulling it out of the tiny hatch. How did Rupert get it up there in the first place?

That mystery would have to go unsolved for the time being.

Sweat oozed down his back as he hurled the television down the hall to the drawing room with only Xavier for help. Poor Flora was too busy to assist because she was serving as a kitchen hand to the merciless kitchen god. James groaned as he reached the top of the stairs. Going backwards, he inched down the stairs one step at a time. His biceps burned under the strain of the LCD television. Xavier simply mumbled as he followed, carrying the other end of the television. The man didn't even break a sweat. He could've at least done the decent thing and pretended to struggle.

Still marching backwards, James inched towards the open door of the sitting room and listened to the laughter and chatter coming from the dining room. James rolled his eyes.

The drawing room was breathtaking. Dark wooden panelling with crossbeams stretched across all four walls. A large four-part casement window spanned the wall to his left. Outside, the storm raged on as he lowered the LCD television onto the floor and opened the box.

The easiest task of the afternoon turned out to be setting up the television and DVD player in the corner of the room.

Quite heroically, after all the heavy lifting was done, Christopher showed up, took one look at the television, and offered to show the unreleased version of his latest film, which was due to premiere in Leicester Square in London in two weeks. He then suggested he could do a question-and-answer session and talk about the filmmaking process. *What an ego.*

To James's surprise, everyone seemed pleased with being confined to a room with that vain cretin. *Is everyone going mad?*

He was trapped in a beautiful manor house with a killer and a bunch of Christopher Page fans. And he was about to search the house with an elderly man.

But before he resumed snooping, he wanted to return to the attic and see if he could view the crime scene from a different perspective. There was bound to be a crack or hole in the floor that he could peer through.

———

MUFFLED chatter floated through Clovervale Hall as James unhooked the door in the ceiling then stood back as the ladder unfolded. He took a deep breath and turned to Xavier. Knowing exactly how their conversation would end, he opened his mouth and started the conversation, not because he was hoping to win a fight but to do the right thing. And so he could look Flora in the eye and tell her that Xavier had ignored his warnings and gone with him, anyway.

'There's no need for you to come with me.' James clutched the rung of the ladder, bracing himself for the storm to come.

Xavier's face reddened. *Here he goes.*

'Oh, there is.' Xavier grimaced. 'Who's going to drag your arse out of the attic when you pass out because you're afraid of heights?' Xavier smirked.

James pursed his lips. 'That happened once. We were at the top of Saint Peter's Basilica, and I realised that those three hundred creepy steps we had just climbed were also the way down. You never told me it was going to be that bad.'

Xavier shook his head and muttered, 'I told you.'

'You said there were about a hundred stairs.' James glared back at him. 'And this is different. I'm mentally prepared.'

Xavier beamed. 'I guess we'll see.'

'No.'

'You don't get to decide.'

James rolled his eyes. 'Why don't we go ask Flora what she thinks?'

Xavier pursed his lips. 'Right after we tell Valentine about the way Honey was looking at you during dinner last night.'

James screwed up his face. 'I don't like Honey.'

Xavier smiled. 'But she is into you. And I'm pretty sure Valentine will be interested in that.'

Touché. The man had a cast-iron will and was going into the attic with him.

Glancing up, James ascended the tiny, creepy ladder into the attic. James could feel Xavier's smugness radiating behind him as he struggled to control his trembling hands. *I can do this. It's not that high.*

After that fruitless conversation, there he was at twenty-five minutes past one, commando-crawling through the attic with a man in his seventies and a nosy feline with a severe case of FOMO.

A pair of bright yellow eyes peered back at him in the dark from the far end of the attic. Michelangelo had secured a front-row seat to the action. An angelic glow surrounded the feline. What was that cat up to?

After they'd endured ten long minutes of crawling, the source of Michelangelo's angelic glow had become apparent. The feline was sitting on a hole in the floor. *Typical cat. Find something new then sit on it.*

James swatted the cat away and inched forward. As James drew nearer to the light, he gasped. He glanced across at Xavier in the darkness. 'Someone has created a hole in the ceiling. And that someone was spying on Laurence.'

Xavier nudged James. 'You don't know that for sure. All you know is there is a hole close to the chandelier.'

The room spun as James placed his right eye on the hole and squinted. Through the hole, the crime scene came into view. To the left, lying on the floor with his feet pointing to the right, was the outline of Laurence's body. Someone must have knelt beside his body after he died. Did they take something from the scene before they left? *His phone.*

James surveyed the scene. 'How did you know the hole was near the light?'

'I guessed we were near the centre of Laurence's room,' Xavier whispered. 'It's plausible that someone could have crept up here and made the hole. Maybe someone tall.'

James sighed. 'Maybe they found your pole.'

'That's plausible too.'

As James pulled away from the hole, he hesitated. Lying down on the attic floor, James placed his eye over the hole and stared at the cigarette butt and ashes on the windowsill. James froze. The window was open, and Laurence had been smoking before he died. Someone could have entered through the window while Gordon was delivering the smoothie.

Then James remembered the narrow ledge around the building. And there was only one way in and out of the attic. Therefore, no one could have quickly moved between the attic and Laurence's window. James rolled his eyes at his stupidity, turned around, and crawled towards the hatch at the other end of the attic.

Without warning, the floor gave way. The room spun as James's heart raced. His chest tightened as the off-white carpet of the floor beneath the attic came hurling at him. On the way to meet the floor, James's feet hooked onto a piece of wood, causing him to thrash about in midair. As his body jerked around, his lower back struck a large portion of wood—a ladder

and a secret hatch. Suspended in the middle of the
room, James grabbed the stairs as his chest tightened.
Merde.

NINETEEN

MUCH TO JAMES'S RELIEF, the floor wasn't too far away. Still shaking, he released his grip on the ladder, dropped into the cleaner's closet, and landed on all fours. Standing up, James found himself surrounded by shelves. Above James, Xavier murmured to himself as he peered into the closet.

The three windowless walls behind him were lined with cleaning products, neatly folded linens, and a series of mops and brooms, and a vacuum cleaner standing in a tall alcove next to a set of shelves that contained buckets along the wall near Laurence's room. In a former life, the closet must have been a dressing room or powder room.

James sighed and glanced up at Xavier.

'I had no idea this hatch was here,' the old man said with a shrug. Xavier descended the ladder and lowered himself into the closet.

Gasping for breath, James leaned against the wall

to his left as he faced the locked door. 'So, they can't get out without the keys, which only you and the cleaner possess, right?' James peered at Xavier, who glanced around the room with a shocked expression on his face.

Xavier nodded. 'Yes, our temporary house cleaner, Marjorie, left before the guests arrived.'

James hesitated as he thought through the possibilities. 'Does the cleaner have a master set of keys like you?'

Xavier narrowed his eyes. 'Yes, and she didn't leave them behind. After she left, I checked all the rooms because I wanted to make sure everything was perfect. I was nervous.'

With his heart still racing, an out-of-breath James propped against the wall between the cleaner's closet and Laurence's room. He needed to take a longer break before climbing up the stairs. *How embarrassing. I'm so unfit.*

'And there's no way someone could access Laurence's room via this closet.' James hit the wall with his fist as he leaned against it. 'It seems quite solid.'

Xavier nodded. 'Yes, that's a sensible conclusion. The writing bureau in Laurence's room is permanently attached to the wall. It's the reason there's one in every room. Flora and I wanted a bit of continuity without having a series of identical rooms.'

James nodded as he furrowed his brow. His eyes widened as he felt the wall move a millimetre to the left. 'It's a hidden door.' James pointed at the wall as he stepped back.

A flicker of light shone through a straight crack in the wall. Glancing down, James noticed a few flakes of plaster on the carpet against the wall. Someone had cleaned up the evidence after discovering the entrance. Leaning in to get a closer look, James noticed that around the frame of the secret door, a layer of paint had peeled away. Another reason he should wear his glasses more often.

Hot breath licked against his neck. He jumped. He turned around and came face-to-face with Xavier, who stood closely behind him, staring at the wall. *Merde.*

'So, whoever watched Laurence in the attic was probably in the closet with him. Somehow, they discovered the secret door, then came back and killed him,' James said over his shoulder as he pushed against the wall and opened the door.

TWENTY

OUTSIDE, the winds howled and the rain beat down against the windows; the storm had no intention of letting up. The manor house creaked in protest. James sighed as the heavy door collided with an object.

Laurence.

After several deep breaths, he squeezed through the gap between the wall and the writing bureau. From behind, a light but sharp object tapped his shoulder. Poking out from the narrow gap was Xavier's hand clutching a box of gloves.

'I can't shimmy through the gap,' Xavier groaned. 'My back's aching.'

Twisting his torso, James grabbed a pair of gloves from the box and put them on. The foul, pungent aroma in the air made James's eyes water. Crouching, he reached out and jabbed the four front pockets of Laurence's tweed jacket with two fingers, careful not to disturb the evidence. As he stood, three short whitish-grey hairs were clinging to the tweed and glistened in the dull afternoon light that shone in from the grey clouds outside. James knelt. The hairs were stained with crimson droplets. *Interesting.*

With questions on his mind, James stood and tiptoed around the crime scene before opening and closing drawers. Something within him needed to find Laurence's phone. Even though there was no reception, reading through the device would give James insight into Laurence's life before he came to Clovervale Hall.

'You're making too much noise,' Xavier stage-whispered from within the cleaner's closet.

Ambling around the bed, James reached the other side and repeated the ritual with the second bedside table. Both drawers were empty. Maybe the killer had wanted Laurence's phone too? From across the room, James stared at the writing bureau.

Why didn't I realise there was a secret door when I was in here earlier?

Then he realised he had been too focused on figuring out whether it was suicide or a crime to notice Laurence's legs leaning towards the right. The more sinister option was that the killer was still in the room while James looked at the body. That could explain the note pinned to his wardrobe. But where would they have hidden? James stared at the closet in the room's corner—it was the only logical place.

As he walked over to the dark-stained oak wardrobe, he paused. The bed was neatly made. It was almost perfect, apart from a single flaw. Its duvet and sheets were neatly tucked under the mattress except for one corner—the left one closest to the wardrobe. It was odd. Sheets cascaded from the top of the mattress to the carpet, concealing the polished timber frame of the four-poster bed. He trekked back and lifted the corner of the mattress. Lying underneath was the missing phone.

Maybe he'd disturbed the killer's search for the smartphone and they left through the secret passage moments before James entered the room, leaving the smartphone behind. Maybe they meant to go back for the smartphone at a later time, like during the night while everyone was asleep.

Perhaps they were worried about getting caught or believed I found the phone?

He picked up the smartphone and tapped the screen. It was one of those brand-new models, released at the end of the previous year, with a fingerprint sensor. He struck the button at the top of the device, and the lock screen lit up. Sixty percent of the battery was drained.

Against his better judgement, James strolled around the room, crouched next to Laurence's body, lifted his right hand, and pressed his index finger against the sensor.

A loud click echoed through the stillness of the room. The screen opened, and the text message app came into view. At the top of the screen was a message trail between Laurence and Christopher. James tapped the screen and waited for the messages to load. Once they did, James froze as he read the exchange.

The hairs on the back of his neck stood on end as he read the message.

So, Christopher had murdered Laurence in order to keep his secret—it was him all along. Glancing up from the screen, James listened. The room was quiet, too quiet. A second loud click broke the silence. James peered at the phone. The screen hadn't locked. A dark shadow hung over James and Laurence's body. *Merde. I've been caught red-handed, and Xavier is probably hurt—or worse.*

'Hand over the phone,' a voice from behind him demanded.

TWENTY-ONE

SUNDAY: 2:16 P.M.

JAMES'S BODY trembled as he rose. Still clutching the phone, he held his hands in the air. Sweat dripped down his forehead as he listened to the voice repeat itself. As he spun around, expecting to come face-to-face with the gun-wielding villain, his eyes met Xavier's wild expression.

The door behind the writing bureau was pushed open even farther than before. James couldn't see Christopher in the mirror's reflection in the left-hand corner of the room because the writing bureau blocked his view. So, he was concealed by the desk or was using Xavier as a shield. James was so fixated on combing the crime scene and finding the phone that he hadn't even heard the desk slide over the carpeted floor. *Merde.*

From behind Xavier, a familiar head of ruler-straight black hair came into view. She had disguised her voice quite convincingly.

'Honey?' James lowered his hands as a loud

explosion followed by an orchestral accompaniment echoed through the manor house from the LCD television and DVD player set up in the sitting room.

She pointed the muzzle of the Smith & Wesson at James. 'Hand it over.'

James furrowed his brow. 'You killed Laurence?'

'Just give her the phone,' Xavier moaned.

'Listen to him,' Honey said in a cold, harsh tone. 'Give me the phone.'

'There's nothing on the phone to incriminate you.' James glanced at the locked screen in his hands.

Honey sighed as she trained the gun on Xavier. 'Fine. Let's try this. The gun in my hand is loaded and ready to be fired. If you don't hand over the phone, I'll shoot your college professor. So, hand it over.'

James rolled his eyes. 'Do you expect me to believe that you won't shoot the both of us after you get the phone?'

Honey narrowed her eyes and shrugged.

'I thought so.' James shook his head. 'You answer my questions, then I'll hand over the phone.'

'James.' Xavier squeezed his eyes shut as Honey shoved him to his knees. She lowered the barrel of the gun to Xavier's head.

'Okay, I'll humour you.' She cocked her head and glared at James. 'Neither of you are going to be around for much longer.'

'There's nothing on this phone that could incriminate you. Sure, there are threatening messages but not to you,' James reasoned. 'Why do you want this? What could be on this phone that's so incriminating that you'd kill another two people to possess it? Why don't you put the gun down? We'll forget all about this and tell the police we found him like this.'

Xavier nodded.

Honey sighed. 'Forensics. I'll get caught. Now hand over the phone.'

'What's on the phone? I want to know why I have to die,' James pleaded.

'A sex tape, you fool.' Tears trickled down Honey's cheeks. 'Now hand it over.'

James stepped back. 'How did he get your sex tape?'

'James.' Xavier groaned. 'Just give her the phone.'

James shrugged. 'She's going to blow our brains out, anyway. I for one would love to die knowing why all this chaos took place.'

Honey's brow wrinkled. 'Fine. I came all the way here to reconcile my divorced birth parents. After all these years, I located my birth mother, Eleanor Norrison. A year ago, I started working for her after discovering that she had changed her name to Sybil Curry and had a cooking-and-restaurant-critique blog. It was terrible. So, I helped write all the recipes. Set up a cooking show online, grew her viewership, and taught her how to perform in front of a camera. Then Sybil got back into restaurant critiquing, which the audience loved. She won an award from a prestigious New York cooking school for her cookbook's unique recipes and got a Silver Play Button for reaching one hundred thousand subscribers to her channel. Technically, I won those awards, but I didn't care.' Honey sobbed. 'Because I had my mother back. Then I convinced her to come here after I learned she was married to Gordon and divorced him a year after I was born. While I was in the library writing up another recipe for the blog, Laurence came into the room. For some reason, he hung around and kept interrupting me. Eventually, he realised I was the writer and blogger behind Sybil Curry's blog, and he threatened to tell the cooking school about her deception.'

'What?' James blurted out. 'All of this for an award?'

'There's more!' Honey snapped. 'So, I gave him an offer he couldn't refuse. I hooked up with him in the closet in exchange for his silence, but Laurence filmed me. And insisted that I hook up with him a few more times, and if I didn't, he would upload my tape for the world to see and then tell the school about Sybil. We went back to his room. Laurence left the closet first. Once the halls were quiet, I left the closet then went to his room. Then, my birth father knocked on the door. He saw Laurence looking dishevelled, heard me, and thought it was Sybil in the room with him. After our afternoon tea, my birth parents fought, and he called off their reconciliation, saying it was a big mistake. Sybil was so hurt. And it was all Laurence's fault. I was so embarrassed. That man would never keep his word. I couldn't trust him. My mother's career would be over, and she would never talk to me again, especially if that sex tape got out. She's proud and super conservative. I was going to lose her for a second time. I had to kill him,' she said through a sea of tears. 'So, I excused myself from the table and, on the way out, grabbed Sybil's gun from her bag while my birth parents were still squabbling. I climbed through the attic and entered the room via the secret door. Pleaded with him, but Laurence was an arse and taunted me. He didn't think I would actually shoot him. So, I shot him. I searched the room for the phone but left after hearing the three of you entering the house. But I screwed up. I left with the gun in my hand, on the way out, made a hole in the ceiling by using a screwdriver I found in the ceiling, just in case I needed to check up on the room. Because the attic floor creaks whenever you climb through it, I couldn't go back and plant the gun. Sybil complained to me about hearing a noise in the ceiling after you discovered Laurence's body, so I knew I would get caught.' Honey sobbed.

James's heart sank. 'So, Sybil knows that you're her daughter?'

Honey's porcelain skin flushed a shade of crimson. 'No, I was going to tell them after they reconciled.'

She raised the barrel of the gun towards James. Her hand trembled as she looked down the barrel. 'Sorry,' she murmured.

As she gained control of her trembling arm, Xavier stepped out from behind the writing bureau and hit her across the back of the head with the steel pipe of the vacuum cleaner. Honey's eyes rolled back as she dropped the gun and fell to the side, hitting her head on the writing bureau.

Xavier gasped. 'Thank God you kept that crazy woman talking.'

James raised his eyebrows at Xavier.

He shrugged, still clutching the pipe from the vacuum cleaner. 'Honey let go of me, and I crawled back into the cleaner's closet. That's when I saw this.' Xavier shook the pipe. 'My back, knees, and neck all ache now. I'm definitely not as young as I used to be.'

James smiled. 'I don't think Honey will wake up soon. Do you have the master set of keys?'

Xavier sighed. 'They're in the kitchen with Flora.'

Ambling around the obstacle course of evidence, James sighed as he mentally prepared for his third trip into the attic.

'I'll be back soon.' James patted Xavier on the back as he stepped into the secret doorway and disappeared into the closet.

TWENTY-TWO

SUNDAY: 2:46 P.M.

STANDING IN THE ENTRANCE HALL, James unlocked the door as he glanced out the large window that looked out onto the courtyard. The loud film score echoed down the hall and almost drowned out the rustling of popcorn. A table umbrella that had already tipped over earlier in the day was rolling around the back lawn. The violent winds and resulting debris had torn apart the hedge maze. James sighed.

Thirty minutes had passed since he relayed the news to Flora and Gordon in the kitchen and retrieved the keys to release Xavier from the room. Together, they decided not to tell the other guests until they contacted the police. To James's surprise, Gordon offered to check the phone lines in the basement. Upon returning to Laurence's room, James discovered Xavier had had a change of heart and wanted to stay with Honey and the vacuum cleaner pipe, just in case she woke up. No matter how much he pleaded, Xavier insisted on staying. He wasn't looking forward to sharing that news with Flora.

Gordon reemerged from the hall that led to the east wings of the manor house, panting. James released his grip on the door handle.

'The underground phone lines in the basement have been severed. The damage can only be repaired by an engineer,' Gordon rasped. 'There's no point going to the phone-line cabinet down the end of the street.'

James raised his eyebrows. 'I thought you said the roads were flooded.'

The chef sighed. 'It was a white lie I told because I wanted to stay and spend time with my daughter.' Gordon frowned. 'And her mother, I guess.'

James rolled his eyes. 'So, we could've walked into town and got help.'

Gordon strolled across the room and placed his hand on the door. 'Are you mad? Have you seen the storm? It's dangerous. Look at that debris. It will kill you.'

Gazing out the window near the door, James watched the heavy rain and violent winds. Thunder crackled. The risk didn't bother him. Nothing seemed to matter after the ordeal with Honey. James turned the handle of the back door and stepped out into the weather, clutching the master key to the pool area.

The icy rain beat down on him and soaked through his light jumper and business shirt as he dashed across the courtyard, weaving between the overturned outdoor furniture. Wet blades of grass squished underfoot as he picked up his pace and sprinted through the hedge maze. For the moment, he was shielded from any rolling table umbrellas or other debris.

As the maze ended, James put his head down and ran to the pool and spa pavilion.

A few minutes later, James found the right key, entered the pavilion, and made his way to the back of the building and the massage parlour. Thankfully, Xavier had put the keys on the ring in order. After slipping the key into the lock, James twisted the handle and opened the door. He strolled into the waiting room, headed to the antique desk, and picked up the phone.

He smiled as he listened to the dial tone. The trip was worth making, after all. Using the old-style rotary dial, James rang 999 and spoke to the emergency dispatcher.

EPILOGUE
SUNDAY: 6:19 P.M.

THREE AND A HALF HOURS LATER, James stood in the dining room, watching a handcuffed Honey climb into a police car, a frazzled Sybil following closely. Rain pattered on the window. The cyclonic conditions had eased. The dark-grey clouds grumbled.

Michelangelo jumped up on the windowsill, trotted along the length of the window, and brushed up against James, leaving a trail of whitish-grey hairs on his navy-blue polo shirt. So it was he who'd left those hairs on Laurence's tweed jacket before he died. The feline was trying to tell him something, after all.

To the left, a paramedic closed the door to the ambulance. It took the police two hours to assess the scene before allowing the pathologist to place Laurence in a body bag and carry him down the stairs. Clovervale Hall swarmed with police officers, and everyone was confined to a different part of the house, waiting to be questioned. James's time with the police was over for now. At some point, they were bound to show up at his home and ask further questions.

Thankfully, Xavier wasn't hurt, and for once, the police weren't suspicious of him. Honey had been arrested for murder. James picked up Michelangelo and cradled the cat in his arms.

A rhythmic tapping caused James to turn around. The door opened, and in walked Xavier wearing a jumper and trench coat.

'Are you thinking about Laurence or Honey?' Xavier stumbled around the dining table.

James sighed. 'Why did he blackmail Honey about writing Sybil's recipes? And then film her in the closet? It's so vile.'

Xavier nodded as he stroked Michelangelo, who purred in James's arms. 'Laurence was always a jealous man. Awards were significant to him. He would've been appalled by Sybil using a ghostwriter.' Xavier nodded. 'That's essentially what Honey was to Sybil, a ghostwriter. And Laurence would have taken the rule-breaking seriously. He would've notified the cooking school. Public announcements would've been made, and Sybil would've been humiliated on the internet and forced to go off-grid and start over again.'

'Yeah, but that's not Honey's fault.'

Xavier shrugged. 'I think Sybil would've blamed her and fired her. Then distanced herself if Laurence released that horrid video.'

James paused. A lone thought entered his mind.

'He was sexually exploiting Honey to make Stella jealous.'

'Making Stella jealous is a pointless task,' Xavier scoffed. 'Stella knows that her marriage to Christopher is PR. She gets fame and gets to hurt Laurence because he injured her pride. But his decision to sexually exploit Honey is a level of evil that I, too, didn't think Laurence would stoop to. James, I don't think you're going to understand why Laurence made the decision to exploit Honey. It was probably spur of the moment, and he didn't think through the consequences. Laurence could be quite blind to consequences when he was enraged about something.'

Together, they stood gazing out the window, watching another police car arrive as the ambulance pulled out of its parking space and drove towards the gates. Laurence had played a dangerous game of cat and mouse, and James wondered what would have happened if Laurence hadn't come across Honey writing more recipes. Maybe he would still be alive. Or maybe Christopher would have resorted to violence to hide his secret.

SUSPICION

JAMES LALONDE AMATEUR SLEUTH MYSTERIES, BOOK 1

Curious about what happens next? If so, check out the first three chapters of the first book in the James Lalonde Amateur Sleuth Mystery Series.

ONE

SUNDAY: 11:38 P.M.

ELIZABETH STAGGERED through the front door and let it swing shut behind her. A sharp pain shot through her head as the loud bang broke the silence in the apartment. Her long, thin fingers brushed against the smooth wall to her left, but nothing was there.

Wrong way, stupid.

She patted the wall, then realised light would only make things worse. Not only would it add a new level of intensity to her headache, but the light would also highlight the thin layer of dust along the skirting boards, the dirty dishes in the kitchen sink, and the clothes lying over the turquoise ottoman at the end of her bed. These were all things she had promised to take care of last weekend, and the clutter was visible the second she opened the front door.

Admitting defeat, she turned around and toggled the deadbolt latch. Her heels clacked against the wooden floorboards as she walked down the dark hall of her apartment, just as she had every evening. The blackout curtains she had purchased a few days earlier were having the desired effect. If only they would help her sleep. As she inched up the hallway toward her bedroom, Elizabeth ran her fingers along the wall.

She paused, and the walls spun around her. She was drunker than she'd thought. Now she was lightheaded, disoriented, and in the dark. Her financial troubles and any plans of late-night research were on hold. She needed to sleep this off.

Earlier that evening, she'd had dinner with the curators of the British Museum. The evening was a complete disaster. These dinners were about networking and securing funds for the next phase of the archaeological dig at Tintagel, but all she had achieved was no funds, more research, and a headache.

Nine months had passed since she'd returned from Cornwall. Sifting through soil and finding fragments of a bygone world was her favourite part of the job. Not that she didn't love research, but it was often challenging. Money always ran out during the research-and-analysis phase of a dig, meaning that she had to raise more funds. This fundraising took time away from research, creating a vicious cycle.

She was fortunate that the Northampton Museum of Anthropology had funded the initial stage of the dig, but the museum was niche and small, not a bottomless pit of cash. The museum had a small number of investors and received government funding on the side. With this allocation of funds came the requirement to justify how the recipient's time and money were spent. That was the thing about investors. They all had the same goals: a high return, low risk, and quick results. It was up to her to find another way to raise funds and to continue the research. But she couldn't do anything tonight.

Leaning against the wall for support, she inched closer to her open bedroom door, stumbled through the doorway, and threw herself onto her bed. As she gazed up at the white space above, her hairpins poked into her scalp. Elizabeth shook off her red patent heels and pulled at her hair. A slight smile formed on her ruby lips as the sharp digging sensation subsided.

She thought about changing into something more comfortable, but any attempt to unzip her dress would only cause her to become dizzier. The room had stopped spinning and she wasn't prepared to upset that delicate equilibrium. Her straightened, but normally curly, black hair fell across her golden-brown skin as she continued to pull the pins out. As she fixed her dark-brown eyes straight ahead, her heavy eyelids closed.

———

PRESSED up against the wall of the dining room, Pippa Baker hung back in the shadows, clutching a black bag and waiting for Elizabeth to go about her night-time routine. She heard movement coming from somewhere within the apartment and, in an attempt to decipher the location of the sound, turned her ear towards the wall between the dining room and the hallway.

Elizabeth must be home.

Pippa was petite and had long brown hair. She had moved from Cambridge, Massachusetts, to Northampton to start a master's degree programme and gain experience in archaeology. She had met Elizabeth on the first day of her internship.

After a few moments, Pippa walked across the hallway to Elizabeth's home office. Elizabeth had a habit of taking her work home with her. This habit made Pippa's next task all too easy. Pippa navigated around Elizabeth's desk at the centre of the room and paused to admire the three framed paintings of the French chateaux at Pierrefonds, Comtal, and Chantilly.

Journals, textbooks, and several PhD theses—all marked with sticky notes—stood in tall piles across the archaeologist's white-stained oak desk. A white bookcase spanned the right-hand side of the room, creating an L shape towards the door. Rows of books, all on just two topics—anthropology and archaeology—lined the shelves.

Enclosed in a long glass box on the bookshelf was a Celtic sword. Pippa walked to the bookshelf and placed her black bag on the floor. Brushing her hair over her shoulder, she lifted the lid of the glass box and pulled out the sword, careful not to cut herself on its broken blade. The long, thin handle glistened in the moonlight that shone from between the thick curtains as Pippa stared at the old Cornish inscription. She knelt down, picked up her black bag, and pulled out a long piece of white linen. After neatly wrapping the Celtic sword, she placed it inside the bag.

Pippa knew it was a bad career move to steal an artefact and sell it to a private buyer. In the archaeological world, it earned the culprit a certain reputation. If caught, she would need to find a new profession. As a teenager, she had dreamed of becoming an archaeologist and excavating in the beautiful deserts of Egypt. But that was all just a fantasy. A childish fantasy. The reality of modern archaeology was so different from the image she'd created in her mind.

As she closed the glass case, she heard furniture scraping against the wall. Pippa froze.

Shit, she must be awake.

Her eyes widened, and her heart raced as she listened to the movements, hoping Elizabeth wouldn't come into her office. But it was useless to panic. There was only one logical thing to do.

Pippa tiptoed up the hall towards the main bedroom. She paused and looked over her shoulder. Tiny hairs on the back of her neck stood on end. No one was there. She wasn't superstitious or easily spooked, but she could have sworn someone was watching her. She knew it. Perhaps the adrenaline rush of the break-in had heightened Pippa's senses and caused her to become paranoid. Besides, it wasn't a break-in if someone had the key, she'd reassured herself as she planned every detail of this operation.

Pippa refocused her attention towards the open bedroom door at the end of the hall.

What is she doing?

As she reached the bedroom, she saw the source of the loud snoring. It was coming from the next room, the living room. The light from the moon pierced through the tiny crack between the thick, heavy curtains, highlighting Elizabeth. She was lying on the sofa with her mouth wide open and a pair of red heels lay scattered across the room. She was still in the same black dress she'd left the museum in over ten hours ago.

Pippa lifted an eyebrow and cocked her head to the side as she clutched the bag close to her chest. On the couch, Elizabeth was stirring. Pippa held her breath as she watched Elizabeth wheeze and gurgle then roll onto her side. She needed to get out of there before Elizabeth woke up. She looked down at the sleeping archaeologist then stepped into the shadows, away from the light.

As she plotted her exit, Pippa once again felt that she wasn't alone. It was as if she had an audience watching her every move. She froze. She turned around, half expecting to see someone standing in the doorway between the hall and the living room. No one was there.

Don't panic.

That was the last thing she needed to do, to panic.

With heightened senses and anxiety came mistakes. Right now, she had to focus. Pippa needed to get out of there before Elizabeth woke up.

Pippa gasped as she felt the coolness of a sharp blade thrust into her back. She looked to her left. In the reflection of the darkened television screen was the outline of a dark figure standing behind her. So, she wasn't paranoid.

Pippa dropped the black bag and pressed her hand against her chest, struggling to breathe. As she fought for air, she felt a sharp pain as the knife was pulled out and her lungs filled with blood. The room spun, and the carpet of Elizabeth's living room drew nearer by the second. What hurt most was the betrayal. Worst of all, she hadn't seen it coming until it was too late.

TWO

———

JAMES LALONDE DROPPED his keys into the small bowl on top of the dark wooden shoe cabinet next to the front door. A little chirp cried out from the smartphone in his pocket. More work, the perfect way to spend the last twenty-two minutes of his Sunday evening.

Valentine is going to scream at me.

That was how every Sunday evening played out. He expected this weekend to be no different. Piles of editing and an angry girlfriend screaming at him in French.

As chief editor of the *Northampton Tribune*, James had a mountain of work to climb and would never reach its summit. He sighed. This was not the job he had wished for as a fresh-faced student. He had dreamed of investigative journalism and the same clichéd fantasies every journalism student imagined: writing in war zones, uncovering government secrets, and exposing corruption. And maybe one day, when he was too old to chase down stories, he would become the chief editor of a newspaper. He'd received his wish, but it had come thirty years too early. And now he longed for the adrenaline rush that came with chasing a story.

James walked down the hall and dumped his bag on the chair at the end of the kitchen table. He pulled out his phone and stared at the screen—he needed to assess the damage. Two messages had come through. The first was his best friend Liam wanting to catch up, and then there was the second. As usual, Harry Lancaster, the owner of the Northampton Tribune, wanted to Skype about the layout of page one. On James's first day as editor, Harry had promised to guide him through his new role. After a year, Harry would step back and observe the paper from afar. Three years later, and this was the man's idea of stepping back. But James had expected that. Harry had the reputation of being hands-on and epitomised the Oxford dictionary's definition of micromanagement.

He sighed as he continued to stare at his screen. Out of the corner of his eye, he noticed a handwritten envelope with his name on it on the kitchen table.

A large stone formed in the pit of his stomach as he recognised the handwriting. He looked around the room and listened to the silence of the house.

'Valentine,' he called out into the emptiness, but he got no response.

Silence was never a good sign, especially from

Valentine. He had expected her to lecture him about his work addiction the second he stepped through the front door. But this evening was different. He was all alone.

He took a deep breath, reached out, and slid the envelope towards him. He stared at the ink on it. A chirp cried out from his phone and disrupted the silence. He rolled his eyes. Another message had come through with one more item to add to his never-ending to-do list.

The handwriting was perfect and neat. It was as if Valentine had taken her time and not written it in a last-minute rush. She loved writing letters and had attended many calligraphy courses throughout their relationship.

This letter seemed different, though perhaps it was his overactive imagination. There was only one way to find out.

James opened the envelope, careful not to tear the letter within. Inside was a single ivory page with Valentine's message.

THREE

AS HE READ the elegant script, the faint smell of Valentine's perfume—a remnant of where her wrist had brushed the paper—took James's mind to a cold winter's afternoon three years earlier. It was January. The sun had already set, and a chilly wind howled through the platform as James wrapped his arms around Valentine's waist and drew her closer. Her eyes reminded him of new, green shoots on the first day of spring. There was something slightly hypnotic about them.

'I hate this train station. Too many bad memories,' he said with a smile as he bent to kiss her ruby-red lips.

Valentine twisted her knotted blonde hair around her neck and down her right shoulder. 'It's saying goodbye every week for the last three months that makes this hard.'

'I know.'

She reached up and kissed him on the cheek.

'Maybe I could talk to my editor and get you a position at the paper. He's always up to his eyeballs in work, and I'm sure he'd find you something. It might be a junior position, but you could move in with me so expenses would be low. That way, we wouldn't have to spend our Sunday evenings in this horrible station.'

James took a deep breath and pulled Valentine a little closer.

Her cheeks flushed dark crimson as she bit the inside of her lip and stared at the ground. 'So, you're springing this on me now, on the platform, one minute before my train leaves for London?' She looked up into his sparkling blue-green eyes.

'Hey, you hate working at the Standard.'

'James—'

'I realise the timing isn't brilliant. But I was meaning to ask you all weekend. Actually, I planned to ask you on Friday night, but I was worried you would say no.'

'So that was the reason for the romantic dinner.'

'Maybe. But every time I tried to raise the subject, you reminded me I'm not allowed to talk about work at the weekends.'

'But in answer to your question, yes, I'd love to work at your paper.' Valentine moved her hand up James's chest and around his neck, leaned in, and kissed him. 'I've got to go.'

She slipped into the carriage as the doors closed and the train rolled out of the station.

JAMES STARED OUT THE WINDOW, the ivory piece of paper drifting towards the floorboards. A tear trickled down his cheek. He gasped as a lone thought swirled around in his mind, jolting him back to reality. As he turned and sprinted up the stairs towards the main bedroom, James slammed the vibrating phone onto the polished tabletop. Another message had come through.

The door handle banged against the wall as James burst into the bedroom. He dived straight for the small, round, black knobs on Valentine's side of the closet. He thrust the doors open and stared at the empty void before him. A space once overflowing with clothes was now bare. His trembling hands slammed the doors shut. He turned around and walked towards the chest of drawers and opened the top ones.

They were empty.

As he closed them one by one, his eye caught the framed picture resting on top of the dresser. He grabbed it with one hand as his legs gave way and he collapsed onto the bed. Tears streamed down his cheeks, falling onto the picture of him and Valentine taken on the steps of the Northampton Museum of Anthropology, a memento from their first year together. James caught the reflection of his reddened eyes in the glass, threw the picture aside and, ran down the stairs towards the kitchen.

He picked up his phone, swiped his finger across

the screen, and listened to the dialling tone. 'The number you have called is not available. Please try again later,' a robotic voice called out of the handset.

'She's left me,' he whispered.

James stabbed the red button to end the call. He sighed as a Skype video call rang through to his phone. *Merde, it's Harry. I have to answer this.*

James Lalonde Amateur Sleuth Mysteries

James Lalonde thought his days of stumbling into murder cases ended with his rookie reporter years. Five years later, as a seasoned editor, he's wrong. From stolen legendary swords to missing manuscripts, James discovers that trouble follows him everywhere, and someone has to solve these crimes.

The Locked Room (Prequel)

It's the opening of Clovervale Hall, an exquisite bed-and-breakfast in England. James Lalonde has an all-expenses-paid trip. But there's one thing he didn't count on—a killer roaming the halls. Soon, James discovers everyone has secrets worth killing for. Can he uncover the truth before the killer strikes again?

The Last Exhibit (Prequel)

When Will Thatcher doesn't show up for work, James Lalonde must attend afternoon tea at the Carmichael Estate. The pleasant gathering ends abruptly when a body is discovered on the front lawn with strange markings on its neck, and a priceless Van Gogh is missing from the wall.

Suspicion (Book 1)

When James Lalonde's girlfriend leaves him, he's forced to cover her story about the local museum's latest acquisition— the legendary sword Excalibur. But when he arrives, Excalibur is missing and there's a dead body at the crime scene. Can James clear his name and find the real killer?

Duplicity (Book 2)

James Lalonde's university reunion takes a deadly turn when a hooded figure murders a professor and steals a priceless mediaeval manuscript, moments after James discovers a secret code within its pages. With his passport confiscated and everyone hiding secrets, can James find the killer before they strike again?

Rookie Reporter Series

Five years before James Lalonde discovered that the legendary sword, Excalibur, was stolen from Elizabeth's flat, he was a gofer dreaming of writing his first byline. The Rookie Reporter mystery series follows James's first year as a journalist, starting with his first-ever case.

The Reporter at the Gate (Book 1)

Rookie reporter James Lalonde finally gets his first story - a simple interview with soon-to-be magistrate Albert Harrington. But when he arrives, he finds blood, an empty safe, and no body. With Detective Khan suspecting him of murder, James must clear his name and solve the case before losing his story.

The Woman in the Lake
(Book 2) - Coming Soon

James Lalonde thought being a groomsman at his ex-girlfriend's wedding would be the most awkward part of his weekend. He was wrong. After the bride's body is found floating in the château's lake, he becomes the prime suspect, and awkward becomes deadly. Can James clear his name before the killer strikes again?

THANK YOU!

There's an old saying that says, "It takes a village to raise a child," the same is true of writing and publishing a story, no matter its size. And this novella is no exception.

Firstly, thank you to Dean Wesley Smith, who, through a series of courses, helped make writing fun for me again. And I couldn't have written this novella without his courses and the writing prompt at the end of the Writing Locked Room Mysteries course. So even though you'll never read this—thank you.

Thanks to my alpha reader, Eric, whom I stumbled across on Fiverr, of all places, for your knowledge and witty comments on my revised draft. You also gave me an idea for a joke which I think is hilarious, reminded me of a bit of history, which I couldn't resist adding to the story, and almost talked me into writing a short story from the point of view of Michelangelo, Xavier's grey cat. Again, I'm unsure if you meant to make me laugh, but you did. And you helped me to create a more realistic story. Your input was, once again, invaluable.

Thank you to my line editor Angela who helped me perfect the prose of this story. She diligently read every word and line several times and gave me feedback I needed to hear.

And last but not least, thank you to my proofreader, Laura for finding those last-minute errors.

Like all those other books I've written, another huge thank you goes to my mother for reading another one of my stories and enthusiastically loving every word.

The novella you just read was the result of a lockdown purchase I made in 2021. While some were making babies, I was buying courses by Dean Wesley Smith, and in particular, a course on Writing Locked Room Mysteries. At the end of that course, Dean shared a writing prompt which, as you can guess, was to write a locked room mystery featuring a cat with less than five thousand words. As I reached the twenty-five percent mark in the first draft, I remembered the cat writing prompt. Because of my cat allergies, I took advantage of the wish fulfilment element of writing, and thus Michelangelo was created.

It'll come as no surprise to you that I couldn't stick to the word limit, and the short story took on a life of its own and became the novella you just read. I hope you had as much fun reading this story as I had writing it—this novella was the most enjoyable hundred and sixteen hours of writing I've had in quite a long time.

But I suspect it only took you a few short hours to enjoy it.

Clovervale Hall and Clovervale Village

Those of you who are anglophiles will be disappointed to learn that Clovervale Hall and its surrounding village are not real. But the manor house is heavily inspired by Polebrook Hall, situated on the south side of Northamptonshire in the charming village with the same name. This is where I got the idea of naming the estate after the village. And Polebrook Hall, which is a private residence, does, upon first look, give off the impression that certain parts of the house were made in a different time period than others. The sad point I'm trying to make is that the estate is private and, at the time of publishing, is not open to the public and is also not found in Oxfordshire. I'm sorry, but I took quite a bit of creative licence in this novella.

More Nostalgia

Perhaps it's my age showing, but I took a few trips down memory lane in The Locked Room. Those who know me will not be surprised by the appearance of the iMac G3 with the matching transparent monitor, keyboard and circular mouse. In my early twenties, this was the very first Apple Mac I used, and since then, I was in love. To this day, I'm still an avid Apple fan, much to the dismay of my Android-loving Husband, although he does have a MacBook.

Don't Look Down

The year my husband and I got engaged, we went on a trip to Italy. This is pre-pandemic, back when travelling with fun and free of swabs—those were the days. My husband and I went to the Vatican for the first time and booked tickets to tour Saint Peter's Basilica. As we booked the tickets, I kid you not; my husband told me there were only one hundred steps to the top of the dome—infamous last words. We exited the lift and then ascended the stairs towards the dome. After climbing a few hundred steps towards the dome, I saw a sign I would never forget. The sign said I was halfway to the top, and there were over one hundred and fifty steps. At that time, I also realised that the creepy stairs I had just climbed were, the way down.

Let's just say I was terrified. Eventually, we reached the top, and I couldn't even look out at the horizon. I was officially afraid of heights. And what about my husband, you ask? He had the time of his life wandering around the top of the dome admiring the view. Meanwhile, I was psyching myself up for the way down. To add a sense of depth and realism to James, I gave him this same fear, but instead, he passed out in his experience.

I know; I'm a monster.

My Favourite Board Game

While we're on the topic of trips down memory lane and nostalgia, in this novella, I included a reference to a board game—the Winter Edition of Carcassonne. This game is, in fact, a real game, but it is a limited edition and is out of circulation. If you're curious about the game, I've included photos of the game on my Instagram and the behind-the-scenes blog post over on my website that relates to this book.

———

Got a burning question about James Lalonde? If so, then check out my FAQ page on my blog at:

authoradhay.com/about/faq/.

ABOUT THE AUTHOR

A. D. Hay is a passionate bibliophile and can usually be found reading a book, and that book will most likely be a murder mystery. She is the author of the *James Lalonde Amateur Sleuth Mystery* and the *Rookie Reporter Amateur Sleuth Mystery* series.

When not absorbed in a gripping page-turner or writing her James Lalonde series, she is a board game addict, loves to travel around Europe, drink tea and rosé, and eat pizza. She is obsessed with journalism, art history and is a closet religious thriller fan.

Born in Brisbane, Australia, she has spent more than a decade in London, where she lives with her husband.

———

You can sign up for a free mystery, The Last Exhibit, behind-the-scenes updates, and bookish research at: authoradhay.com/read-free/

amazon.com/author/adhay

bsky.app/profile/writeradhay.bsky.social

bookbub.com/authors/a-d-hay

facebook.com/AuthorADHay

goodreads.com/authoradhay

instagram.com/writeradhay

threads.com/@writeradhay

tiktok.com/@authoradhay

x.com/WriterADHay

youtube.com/@AuthorADHay